PATHS OF DEATH

He had done with killing. That was all in the past. Zacchaeus Wolfe was a peaceful dirt farmer. But the Lazy K didn't like sodbusters. The Kerfoots owned the range . . . and the law. His little farm did not fit into their plans. So old man Barrett Kerfoot and his five sons, backed by a full complement of cowboys, began to push Zacchaeus. But they'd find out the hard way what it was to have a curly wolf by the tail . . .

g. MAR

Please return / renew by date shown.
You can renew it at:
norlink.norfolk.gov.uk
or by telephone: 0344 800 8006
Please have your library card & PIN ready

A

Finch

ROTATION
PLAN

NORFOLK LIBRARY
AND INFORMATION SERVICE

P. McCORMAC

◆

PATHS OF DEATH

Complete and Unabridged

LINFORD
Leicester

First published in Great Britain in 2008 by
Robert Hale Limited
London

First Linford Edition
published 2010
by arrangement with
Robert Hale Limited
London

British Library CIP Data

McCormac, P.
    Paths of death. - - (Linford western library)
    1. Western stories.
    2. Large type books.
    I. Title II. Series
    823.9'2–dc22

ISBN 978–1–44480–015–9

Published by
F. A. Thorpe (Publishing)
Anstey, Leicestershire

Set by Words & Graphics Ltd.
Anstey, Leicestershire
Printed and bound in Great Britain by
T. J. International Ltd., Padstow, Cornwall

This book is printed on acid-free paper

1

It was a face that had seen hardship and sorrow. Deep furrows were etched each side of his nose to meet with similar deep creases slanting along the side of his face. It was a lean face honed in planes and slants and carved in mahogany. The eyes were deep-set and brooding as if the man was forever looking inwards at some place of bottomless darkness.

He stood immobile like a carved Indian totem pole staring out at the ruined cornfield. Slowly he raised his left arm. Where the hand should have been there was instead a calloused nub of skin. With his good right hand he massaged the mutilated limb.

The fence around the field had been broken in several places. The field looked as if a herd of buffalo had stampeded through it. No emotion showed on that inexpressive face though the field of corn represented many months of hard work. At last he turned to the woman standing with him.

'I might salvage something from the field,' he told her.

His wife was black and tall and lissom. Her hair was gathered up on her head exposing delicate shell-like ears. She had a slim straight nose and high cheekbones. Her eyes were large and liquid with murky, deep-brown pupils. She was very beautiful. Those lovely eyes were cloudy with worry as she stared out at the devastation.

It was not wild buffalo that had wrought the destruction but a herd of longhorns that had trampled through the corn. The longhorns of their own accord might not have breached the fences. There was no reason for them to have come this far. The man who owned the field of corn knew the herd had been driven deliberately into the field. This was not the first time it had happened.

'I'll go into town and inform the sheriff.'

'Zacchaeus, promise me, no trouble.'

'No trouble, Gabrielle,' he said. 'I'll call in Lavinia's. Make sure she and Angelina are all right.'

He saddled up the horse. Gabrielle hovered round watching his every move.

'You sure it was the Lazy K riders?' he asked.

'I watched from the cabin. They hazed those cows up into our field. Roped the fence and pulled out sections of it to allow them through.'

He took no gun. He had promised there would be no trouble. She was afraid of what he would do — what he was capable of.

Consul was a growing town. More and more families were coming in to settle the territory on government land grants.

He stopped by the shop with the sign advertising Lavinia's Fashions. Like most stores on the street it had a high

3

false front. Above the shop a mural had been painted showing a fashionable Paris street scene in which ladies in stylish dress promenaded.

He entered the shop feeling self-conscious in his grubby farm labourer's clothes. A small bell on the door tinkled a warning. He did not venture far inside but stood watching his niece, Lavinia, as she attended a plump matron. She looked up as he entered and gave a warm smile when she saw him. Hearing the doorbell her partner in the business, Angelina, came out to assist.

'Master Zacchaeus.' Angelina had once worked for Zacchaeus Wolfe and could not get out of the habit of addressing him as master. She was a plump, attractive young black woman.

Zacchaeus doffed his hat. 'Angelina.'

'How is Gabrielle?'

'She's fine.'

Lavinia had wrapped the goods for the woman and was escorting her to the door. When the customer was outside she closed the door, turned and hugged her uncle. Releasing him from her fervent embrace she pointed out back and mimed drinking from a cup. Before moving to Consul Lavinia had been injured in a savage attack that left her unable to speak.[1]

'Perhaps I will on the way back. I got business in town.'

Lavinia's lovely young face creased in a frown. She sensed something in her uncle's voice. Taking out a small notebook she wrote out a question for him.

What is it Uncle Zac? Not more trouble?

'You don't miss much, Lavinia. Yeah, had a herd of longhorns trample the corn. I'm on my way to see the sheriff.'

'Sheriff Harrell only has one citizen he provides law for,' Angelina butted in, her voice dripping with scorn. 'That's

---

[1] See, *Zacchaeus Wolfe*, Robert Hale, 2007.

Barrett Kerfoot, the man who owns the Lazy K. I don't know why you waste your time complaining to that lame excuse for a law officer.'

Zacchaeus shrugged. 'I gotta go through the motions. Maybe if Sheriff Harrell gets enough complaints then he might be forced to do something.'

'Don't you hold your breath waiting for that to happen, Master Zacchaeus. When you finished with the sheriff you make sure you come by for a coffee and some of my biscuits afore you leave Consul.'

Zacchaeus put his hat back on his head and smiled at the two women. He glanced around the shop with its lavish display of lady's garments.

'You two seem to be doing OK. I never knew there were so many females in Consul to buy all these here fashions.'

'Our fame is growing. Our clientele is coming from near and far to investigate Miss Lavinia's delights.'

Lavinia smiled and wrote again in her

6

book for Zacchaeus.

It's Angelina's skilful sewing that makes our pieces so desirable.

* * *

Angelina shook her head and grinned delightedly. 'Miss Lavinia she just being kind, Master Zacchaeus. It her good business sense that keep us going.'

Sheriff Saul Harrell was sitting behind his desk reading the *Consul Mercury* when the door opened. Irritated at being interrupted he looked up with a frown that he could quickly turn to a welcoming smile should the intruder be someone of consequence. His frown deepened when he saw the grubby man who pushed into his office.

'Yes,' he snapped. 'What the hell is it this time?'

'I've had more trouble with the Lazy K,' Zacchaeus said mildly. 'They busted my fence and drove a herd of longhorns through my corn.'

Harrell laid his paper on the desk and

massaged his eyes with both hands. When he finished this little exercise he stared with some hostility at the homesteader.

'I was hoping when I opened my eyes again you would be gone.'

'That's three times this month those cowpunchers have driven cattle through my land,' Zacchaeus said ignoring the slight. 'If this goes on I won't have any crops to harvest this year.'

'Mr Wolfe, this is cattle country. Cattle were roaming free around here since before you were born. Just because you put up a few fences don't mean a thing to those longhorns. They just dumb animals, a bit like home-steaders, come to think. Don't know no different. You'll just have to accept cattle roaming about the place just like anything else that's natural. A swarm of locusts might just as well come down on that there cornfield and do far more damage. Them dumb cows don't know you own that land. You should be thankful it were only cows that came onto the cornfield and not locusts. I'm sure the cows would have left you some of your corn whereas a swarm of locusts would have stripped the field bare.'

'What does a man have to do to protect his property if the law won't help him?'

'That's a mighty unfair thing to say, citizen. Cattlemen have rights too, you know. They can't be watching their cattle twenty-four hours a day. They do their best but they's plumb too many longhorns out there to keep corralled. Some of them ornery critters is bounden to stray.'

'In other words you ain't gonna do nothing to upset Barrett Kerfoot, the owner of Lazy K, who pays your wages?'

Anger suffused the porcine features of Consul's lawman. 'Goddamn, I don't have to take that sort of backchat from no damn sodbuster. You watch your mouth, mister, or you might find yourself tossed in jail for a few days to help you cool off!'

'In that case I'll be forced to write to the Governor. Ask if there's a separate law for the rich rancher and a different law for the poor homesteader. It would appear the Constitution of the United States does not extend to Consul.'

'Mister, you keep pushing and you'll end up behind bars. If I chuck you in jail how the hell will your precious crops fare then, with no one to tend them!'

Zacchaeus Wolfe nodded. His deep-set muddy eyes showed no expression. 'I just needed to know where I stand, Sheriff, in the judgment of the law.'

He turned and stepped back out on to the boardwalk and stopped. The half-dozen cowpunchers stood in a semicircle in the roadway. All the men were armed with gun belts and six-guns. In the centre was a tow-haired, handsome youth. His hat was pushed back on his head and he had a mocking grin on his face.

Stewart Kerfoot was the second youngest son of Barrett Kerfoot, the man whose cattle ranch abutted Zacchaeus Wolfe's land, the man who resented homesteaders moving on to Government land.

'Well, looky what we got here fellas,' the youngster sneered, 'a stinking sodbuster coming in our town an' messing it up.'

2

Zaccheus stood very still, arms dangling by his sides, waiting.

'What you doing in town, sodbuster? You should be out grubbing in that stinking homestead of yourn.'

'I came in town to make a complaint to the sheriff. A bunch of Lazy K cows were driven into my cornfield. The men as did it busted my fences at the same time. Maybe I should ride out to the Lazy K and see old man Kerfoot about compensation.'

'Nobody from Lazy K has been near your stinking place. Them cows musta wandered off on their own and got on your place by accident. Can't blame us for that, sodbuster.'

'You were seen uprooting the fences and deliberately driving the cattle on the corn.'

The youngster's face changed then.

His smile disappeared and a hard glint came in his eyes. A hand hovered over his pistol.

'You calling me a liar, sodbuster?'

'You take whatever meaning you want from my complaints.' Zacchaeus spoke in a calm, even voice. 'Now, if you'll excuse me I got business to attend to.'

'Hold on mister!' The youngster put out a hand as if to stop the farmer. 'No one calls a Kerfoot a liar and walks away like that. You either put up or shut up.' All the time he was speaking he kept his right hand clawed above the holstered pistol.

Zacchaeus held his arms away from his sides. 'If you're looking for a gunfight I ain't armed. Now just let me pass peaceable. I don't want no trouble. I came in town peaceable. I intend to leave that way.'

'Mister, you called me a liar. I ain't taking that from no one and especially no stinking sodbuster sonovabitch. Now you got two choices. You either go get yourself a side iron or you get down on your knees right now and say sorry to me and all these hardworking cowboys as you called liars.'

'I have no wish to fight with you.'

'You a low-down coward?' Suddenly the gun was in the youngster's hand. 'If you're not on your knees begging pardon, then I'm gonna pistol-whip some respect into that sodbuster head of yours.'

Zacchaeus stood before the arc of cowboys, showing no emotion. They were grinning in anticipation of the fun they would get from watching their boss beat the sodbuster into the dirt.

Stewart Kerfoot raised his pistol and stepped forward on to the boardwalk.

'One more chance, sodbuster.'

There was no response from the homesteader. He was motionless, almost like he was rooted to the boardwalk, a stump of an old tree waiting to be chopped down. The cowpuncher swung the pistol. He aimed at the man's head. The blow was intended to strike the farmer on the face with sufficient force to drive him to his knees.

Stewart was enraged enough to beat the helpless man to a pulp. His hatred and ire was evident in his twisted face. His friends were watching. He was committed to putting on a good show. He had done it before. As well as beatings, Stewart Kerfoot had two notches on his gun.

One man had been badly wounded and another shot to death. The youngster had never been arrested for either shooting. Stewart acted with impunity under the indulgent eye of his wealthy and powerful father, Barrett Kerfoot and his bought-and-paid-for law officer, Saul Harrell.

The blow never landed. It was checked in midair as the homesteader erupted onto action. The man moved so swiftly the cowboy spectators were not sure how it happened.

Stewart Kerfoot's hand was suddenly clamped in work-caloused fingers. Iron bands closed relentlessly, crushing the youngster's fingers against the hard unyielding metal of his pistol.

He opened his mouth to scream but was cut short as a stump of hardened gristle smashed him between the eyes. The youngster was sagging at the knees when that stump struck again. This time it drove like a piston into his solar plexus. A sideways swipe and Stewart Kerfoot slumped insensible to the boardwalk.

It took seconds for this startling result to register with the remaining cowboys. They went for their guns, and then stopped. Kerfoot's weapon was in the hand of the sodbuster and aimed squarely at the five cowpunchers. The man behind the weapon did not speak. He just stood there holding the commandeered Colt like it had grown into his one good hand.

It was an astonishing reversal of fortunes. Never before had anyone stood up to the bullying tactics of a Kerfoot. There was no challenge from the man standing so implacable before the cowboys, no gloating, and no sneer on his face, no triumph. The weapon he held was rock steady and the cowboys were wrong-footed, unsure, unable to proceed without leadership from their boss.

'You're dead, mister,' one of them spoke at last, almost whispering the words as if afraid to speak any louder in case he might provoke the man with the gun pointed at him. 'If Stewart don't do it his old man Barrett certainly will.'

'I'm walking down the street to my horse. I'll hold on to this gun till I'm out of town. You'll find it on the trail. I never asked for this trouble.'

He strode past them, the gun dangling by his side. The cowpunchers watched him go. Followed him down the street with their hating eyes. He never looked back. They could have pulled their irons and gunned him down now he had his back to them. None of them had the courage to try.

Inside the law office Sheriff Saul Harrell was complacently reading his

17

paper. He had heard the confrontation take place outside his door. There was a smirk on his face. He knew quite well what was happening.

That upstart homesteader was about to learn it didn't pay to come into town and make complaints against the Lazy K. Stewart Kerfoot was in town. The hotheaded youngster would take care of the problem. The Kerfoots had a way of dealing with bothersome sodbusters. There was no need for the sheriff of Consul to interfere. His door was pushed open. He looked up with a knowing smirk as he saw the Lazy K cowboys lugging an unconscious man into his office.

3

Gabrielle looked into his eyes. He turned away thinking she had noticed nothing.

'What is it, Zacchaeus? What happened?'

He should have known better. He could hide nothing from her.

'Those cowboys, they wanted to pistol-whip me.'

'Are they hurt bad?' she asked.

'Just their pride, mostly. It was Stewart Kerfoot. I showed him I had no gun. It was an opportunity to teach me a lesson. I had to swat him into the dirt.'

Delicate worry lines appeared on her elegant forehead. 'And Sheriff Harrell?'

Zacchaeus shrugged. 'He's afraid of the Kerfoots. If he takes action against them he's out of a job.'

'They'll come for you.'

They were standing face to face, hiding nothing from each other. He gazed into her limpid eyes feeling as always the love and tenderness that made him weak and pliant when he was with her. It was also the source of strength between them. No matter how the elements or men bothered them, they had the constant love of each other. That was their strength. Their love for each other kept them strong.

'Zacchaeus, you've not gone hunting since we arrived here. We could do with some venison. Take your rifle and go up in those hills and bring back a deer. Take your time, maybe two or three days. Then come home safe to me.'

She knew when they came they might destroy things, objects that could be replaced or repaired. Her man could not be replaced. If he were here when they rode in he might kill some of them and if that happened he would be hunted to destruction. The fragile life they had hoped to build here in Nebraska would be destroyed. They had to hang on — roll with the punches and wait for the trouble to blow over.

'I'll get you some food. Saddle up a horse. You'll be gone awhile.'

She turned and went inside the cabin. He stared out at the land he had homesteaded. The Kerfoots owned thousands of acres. Ran hundreds of head of cattle. Their own tiny homestead was insignificant in comparison. The rancher was doing everything lawful and unlawful to get rid of them.

Homesteaders were ticks clinging to the hide of a mangy longhorn. The animal was doing its best to rid itself of the pests. It would roll in the mud, scrape itself against fence posts and trees to rid itself of the irritants. But the ticks kept coming. Nothing stopped them. When enough of them invaded, the longhorn took off and ran, maddened by the aggravation. That was what Zacchaeus was hoping would happen. More homesteaders arriving would lessen the pressure on him. He would not be so alone any more.

He saddled his horse, the big black stallion. It had served him well during the war. Now it could take a vacation with its master. Spend some time together in the hills, alone in the woods at night thinking of his lovely wife, Gabrielle and the cosy home they had built.

She came out of the cabin with a bundle of food. He pushed the pack inside his saddle-bags. Turned back and she was in his arms.

'Don't let them catch you, Zacchaeus. I need you safe back here with me.'

He held her tight against him, feeling her breasts warm and soft against his body. She could rouse him with a look.

'I love you, Gabrielle. You take care.'

He swung up into the saddle, gave her a tight smile and set the horse in motion. When he turned back to wave goodbye she was still watching him, tall and straight, standing in the yard. She raised her arm and waved. An immense melancholy overwhelmed him and he almost turned back.

To hell with the Kerfoots! These men had wronged him. This was his home. He had a right to defend himself. It was not in his nature to run.

He turned his face towards the distant tree-clad hills. Gabrielle had told him what he had to do and he knew she was right. Whatever happened he must remain alive and elusive and keep the confrontations to a minimum.

* * *

They caught him only a few miles from home. At first he thought the dust cloud was from another herd of longhorns being driven towards his farm to wreak more havoc. Then the dust cloud resolved into a mob of horsemen riding hard. By then it was too late to avoid a confrontation. He reined up and waited for them.

There were a dozen or more riders. When they saw him they whooped and some hotheads fired shots into the air.

Sheriff Harrell was leading them. By his side was Stewart Kerfoot. The youngster's face was bruised and swollen. He stared at Zacchaeus with malevolent hatred.

'There's the sonovabitch, Sheriff. Arrest him.'

There was a self-satisfied smirk on the sheriff's face as he contemplated the lone rider.

'Wolfe, you're under arrest.'

'Sheriff, what law have I broke?'

'Attempted murder, that's what. You tried to murder young Kerfoot here. I'm taking you in.'

'An unarmed man is attacked by six armed men and when he is forced to defend himself he's accused of murder. It don't seem like no law to me.' Zacchaeus did not raise his voice.

'You'll have a chance to tell it all to the judge, Wolfe. Just keep your hands away from that rifle. I got witnesses here as saw you attack young Kerfoot here without provocation. They had to pull you off him afore you beat him to death. If that ain't attempted murder then I'm no sheriff.'

'You're sure right there, you gutless excuse for a law officer. You know as well as I do these boys are lying. Now if you'll excuse me I have a day's hunting ahead of me.'

They had him boxed in. Convinced their victim would come quietly, they were grinning confidently. There were too many of them for this sodbuster to take on. They were not aware of the nature of the man they were dealing with. The confrontation in front of the sheriff's office when he had disarmed one of the cowboys and faced down his companions should have given them a hint as to his dangerous qualities.

They smirked knowingly as he sat his horse and waited for them to move on him. Only it was Zacchaeus who moved first. He drove in his heels and the big stallion, schooled in war to instant action, plunged headlong towards Sheriff Harrell and Stewart Kerfoot.

4

'Richard, can you take me into town? Your father wants me to go to the bank and I have some errands of my own to attend to.'

'Sure, Ma, where's Stewart? I thought he usually took you.'

'Your brother seems to have plans of his own. I hardly ever see him now. Your pa claims your brother is sowing his wild oats and learning to be a man. As I understand it that means he's out hounding homesteaders or some such activity.'

'Ma, why does Pa have to be so ornery against those poor sodbusters? Surely there's enough land to go round?'

Martha Kerfoot was frowning slightly as she regarded her son and considered his question. In spite of giving birth to five sons she was still a strikingly handsome woman. She had fine expressive eyes and a soft and generous mouth. A mass of auburn hair with little or no silver showing made her seem much younger than her forty-seven years.

Richard Kerfoot was the youngest of her brood. His brother Stewart at twenty-two was three years older. Daniel the next in age was a year older than Stewart. His father had sent him to law school.

'The way things are shaping up with all these sodbusters crowding in we'll need a lawyer in the family to keep those vultures at bay,' Barrett Kerfoot had claimed. 'When Daniel is qualified he can take over all the legal matters for the Lazy K. We should save a fortune on shyster's fees.'

Ethan, aged twenty-five was in charge of the day to day running of the ranch. Paul the eldest was off soldiering. When he had reached the ripe old age of twenty-five he had insisted, against his father's wishes, on joining the army.

There was only another year to go before his five-year stint was up.

Running the Lazy K was a massive task and the old man, Barrett Kerfoot, now in his mid fifties, tough and iron-willed, insisted his boys pulled their weight. He was an unremitting taskmaster and drove all around him as hard as he drove himself. One of his favourite quotes was from from Ecclesiastes.

Whatsoever thy hand findeth to do, do it with all thy might; for there is no work, nor device, no knowledge nor wisdom in the grave, whither thou goest.

'My dear Richard, the question as to why your father follows a certain path is only for your father to answer. So why don't you ask him and not me? I'm only his wife, for God's sake.' His mother waved her hand dismissively. 'I have more important things to occupy my time than your father's motives or your brother Stewart's rampaging. If you ask me, your father is too indulgent with that young scallywag.'

'Ah, Stewart is all right. He'll grow out of it,' Richard surmised.

Martha Kerfoot smiled at her son's condescending tone, thinking that Richard showed a much more mature approach to life than his brother. At nineteen he believed he was the sophisticated young rancher.

The drive to town was uneventful. As they entered the town Martha leaned over to speak to her son.

'Last week I ordered a dress from Lavinia's Fashions. Pull over there in front of the store.'

Richard obediently did as he was told.

'How long will you be, Ma? Will I have time to have a drink down at the Elephant and Monkey.'

Her lips pursed as Mrs Kerfoot made an impatient noise.

'Stewart always came into the store with me. He has good taste, has your brother. He was always on hand to help me.'

She did not see the face her son pulled as she said this. With a resigned look he clambered down and helped his mother to the boardwalk. The small bell tinkled as they opened the shop door. A young woman was standing with her back to them as they entered. She was making adjustments to a fashion gown adorning a dressmaker's dummy. She turned and smiled warmly at the newcomers, inclining her head in greeting.

Richard Kerfoot stared with some interest at the young woman. He assumed she was the shop owner's assistant. Shopkeepers, in his mind, were associated with large formidable women. This was just a young girl waiting to greet his mother.

'Ah, Miss Lavinia,' his mother greeted the girl. 'Good morning, I take it that is my creation you are working on?'

The girl dipped her head in acknowledgement. Richard stared at her. He realized he was mistaken in assuming she was an assistant. From his mother's greeting she was the Lavinia advertised on the shop front. She was certainly much younger than he had imagined and extremely attractive too.

Lavinia was wearing a fine mauve dress that had an exceptionally high black lace top covering most of her neck up to her chin. Her hair was black also and neatly groomed. Soft dark waves coiled back from the sides of her fine face, enhancing its delicate bones. The skin was pale and healthy, while her full lips were red and soft. Richard stared at this vision. He had never seen anything so beautiful.

Mrs Kerfoot moved over to the model and examined the elegant dress. She reached out a hand and tenderly caressed the pleats and ruffles of the garment.

'Miss Lavinia, I do declare you have excelled yourself. Richard, what do you think? Do you like the colour and the style?'

Lavinia turned her attention to Richard, catching him unawares staring in open admiration at her. She smiled and inclined her head graciously. Richard blushed deeply. His mother turned impatiently, saw his blushes and glanced shrewdly from the girl to her son.

'I knew I should have brought Stewart. He's not so empty-headed.' She turned to Lavinia. 'This is another of my sons, Miss Lavinia. His name is Richard. I'm afraid he's more at home in a corral amongst a herd of horses than in a ladies' fashion shop.'

Richard stepped forward. It was only at the last moment he remembered to snatch off his hat.

'How do you do, Miss Lavinia?' he managed to mumble. 'I sure am pleased to make your acquaintance.'

Her smile captivated him and instead of speaking she bowed graciously.

'Richard,' his mother scolded, 'can you stop making cow's eyes at the young lady and look at this dress instead. Really, you are so immature. Men!' She switched her attention back to Lavinia. 'Take them off a horse and they become helpless and infantile. You'll know what I mean if you ever have the misfortune to have children of your own. I have five boys and one husband. It's a full-time job keeping their attention on something that hasn't got four legs and a pair of horns.'

Lavinia smiled indulgently.

'May I try it on before I take delivery? Would that be a lot of bother?'

Lavinia picked up a small brass bell and jangled it. In a moment a young black woman emerged from behind curtains at the rear of the shop. Lavinia signed to the woman, who curtsied towards Martha Kerfoot.

'Come this way, Mrs Kerfoot. The fitting-room is just out back. I'll assist you if you require.'

5

Lavinia, with the black girl helping, carried the dress out through the curtained archway. With an exasperated look at her son Martha swept after them. Richard was left alone with his thoughts for company. He did not have long to wait before Lavinia returned. She smiled over at him and began to busy herself behind the wooden counter.

Left alone with the girl Richard was tongue-tied. Desperately he searched for something to say. The girl did not help his embarrassment. Other than smile at him once or twice she had not uttered a single word. He fumbled with his hat and stared furtively at her.

She was devastatingly beautiful but remote like a being from a different world. She was probably too sophisticated to bother herself with a common cowhand.

If only he could know, Lavinia was acutely aware of his attention. She tried to ignore him by concentrating on tidying bolts of cloth and dusting non-existent motes of dirt from spotless shelves and counter. The young man standing so awkwardly in her shop excited feelings in her she had not experienced for a long time. She knew he was covertly watching her and, aware of this attention, Lavinia became increasingly uncomfortable. Richard realized he had to say something. He took a deep breath.

'Miss Lavinia, this sure is a grand shop. It's a mighty credit to you.'

He was sweating and discomfited as he spoke. She turned her full gaze on him. Her radiant smile made him go weak at the knees. Bravely he stumbled on.

'I . . . I know you must think me a bumbling fool . . . its just I ain't used to being with ladies . . . as least not ladies as purty as you are . . . '

He faltered, not knowing how to

proceed, wishing she would say something, anything to ease his embarrassment. Unaware he was doing so, as he spoke he had moved closer. Only the width of the counter separated them. He stared hopelessly at her. And in that moment as they gazed into each other's eyes something moved in her eyes, something lost and lonely. He had a sensation of a forlorn soul reaching out to him, craving understanding. It touched him to his heart and he was lost in the depth of emotion he was sensing in her eyes.

'Richard, what do you think?'

He started and dragged his eyes away from those deep pools of longing. The moment was lost. He was back with his mother in a dress shop.

Lavinia bustled from behind the counter and approached his mother, now attired in the new dress. He gulped as he tried to gather his confused feelings.

'Sure is purty, Ma. I never saw anything so purty.' He wasn't looking at his mother; he was staring at the back of Lavinia's head as he spoke.

They were on their way back at the Lazy K before Richard had the courage to broach the subject to his mother.

'Miss Lavinia seems awful young to own a dress shop, Ma.'

'I don't think she's that young,' Martha said sharply. 'Anyway you have to take pity on the poor creature seeing as she's a dummy.'

'A dummy . . . how do you mean, Ma?'

'She's dumb! Can't speak, that's what.'

'Oh . . . I . . . didn't know.' Richard was beginning to understand why Lavinia had not spoken. Somehow her affliction made him feel protective and loving towards her. 'A person as can't speak is a mute, Ma. Dummy is a bit crude.'

'Like your pa I call a spade a spade. Lavinia the dressmaker is a dummy no matter how you want to dress it up.'

'No dummy could run a successful

business as she does.'

Martha Kerfoot was smiling mockingly at her son's discomfort. 'So, Richard dear, what would you call her exactly?'

'She's a real lady, Ma. A woman as runs her own business ain't what you just called her.'

Martha moved closer to her son. She put out her hand and placed it on his shoulder. Richard took after his mother with stunning good looks. He had her dark wide-set eyes and full sensual lips. Curly auburn hair fell over his fine deep forehead in an untidy jumble.

'Son, she's flawed. A woman without all her faculties is not good stock for a Kerfoot. Forget the poor maimed creature. Look for a woman more in keeping with our family values.'

Richard flushed even deeper red. 'I . . . uh . . . Ma, I weren't thinking of her in that way.'

They drove the rest of the way home in silence. When they arrived at the Lazy K ranch house Richard handed his mother down from the buggy and quickly led the vehicle towards the stables.

Martha Kerfoot stared thoughtfully after her son. Of all her boys he was her second favourite. Because of his wild and mischievous ways, Stewart was her pet. She loved him above all her children. But Richard, because of his gentle nature and good looks, lay next in line for her affection.

'Lavinia's Fashions . . . ' she said thoughtfully. 'I trust it's just a passing fancy.'

His mind still churning over the remarks his mother had aimed at the lovely young woman he had met in Consul, Richard Kerfoot headed for the corral. His favourite mare saw him coming and gave a short whinny of pleasure. She trotted to the fence and pushed her nose through the bars in expectation of a treat. Richard stroked her velvety muzzle for a moment. Her lips puckered in anticipation as he pushed his hand inside a pocket and pulled out a few sugar lumps.

'Ah, Barley, I can talk to you about the angel I met in town today,' he said as the mare eagerly sucked up the sweet titbits.

He climbed the corral rails and jumped inside. The mare whickered her pleasure and pushed hard against her master. Appreciatively he ran his hand along her back. He gazed fondly at the horse.

'It's like this, Barley. Ma asked me to take her into town. She went into Miss Lavinia's to look at some fabrics. Before today I'd never been in that there shop. Ma wanted my opinion about the colour or some such thing. As if I know anything about ladies' wear. Anyway, Miss Lavinia was there. She smiled at me. Barley, I tell you now, she had the most perfect face I've ever seen.'

As he spoke Richard was fondly stroking the mare. She was pushing against him, nuzzling at her favourite person. Richard had a habit of speaking to his horses. His voice was soft and soothing and the animals loved him back.

'Her eyes, they were like bright stars that would shine on a moonlit night. There was like a sorta luminous glow to them and when she looked at me I sorta felt weak at the knees.'

The mare was staring up at her master in adoration. He smiled at her.

'You know, Barley, I've just had a great idea. I'm thinking there's a lady as might just appreciate my favourite mare as a special gift.'

6

Sheriff Harrell jerked hard at the reins of his mount in an attempt to pull away from the big stallion coming at him at the speed of a steam train and seeming just as large and menacing. He partly succeeded in getting out of danger till the stallion hit the rear end of his own horse, making it rear in fright. The lawman was thrown from the saddle, He fell from his mount screaming in fright as he tumbled to the dirt. The next few minutes of frenzied action were lost to him as he rolled frantically from under the feet of his terrified horse.

Stewart Kerfoot had been beside the sheriff, revelling in this moment of triumph. When the stallion bounded forward he grabbed for his Colt. Suddenly the horse and rider were upon him. A rifle butt came out of the blue and smashed into the side of his head. Stewart went back over the rear of his cowpony, losing his grip on his weapon.

There was a sudden explosion of shots as the posse fired wildly at the fleeing horseman. If he had only been faced with a bunch of townsmen Zacchaeus Wolfe might have succeeded in his wild bid for freedom. However the posse was made up mostly of Lazy K cowboys. Most were drunk and had been wound up by their young boss.

Stewart had told them of the cowardly attack on him. It was unthinkable a Kerfoot should be treated with anything other than respect. But worst of all, the assailant had been a sodbuster, the most reviled and lowest of all God's creatures.

Some of the drunken cowboys already had their guns out as they confronted the sodbuster. They began firing wildly at the fleeing horseman. It took only one lucky shot. Low and hard a bullet smashed into the stallion's lower leg. The mighty beast stumbled as the bone was smashed. It tried to favour the leg and keep it off the ground. It was a doomed effort. Instead of an ironshod hoof hitting the ground, fractured bone smashed down with fearful consequences. Instantly the stallion went down screaming as the leg crumbled beneath it.

Zacchaeus, not realizing what had happened to his mount, hauled on the reins in a vain effort to maintain the stallion's equilibrium. Then he was desperately trying to pull his feet from the stirrups as the horse went down. Before the great beast hit the ground Zacchaeus was thrown clear and slammed into the ground with a bone jarring thud. He was twisting round from his prone position trying to see what had happened to his beloved stallion. Then riders were milling round him blocking off his view. They were yelling and pointing weapons at him. He lay in the dirt staring up at them and hearing his stallion screaming.

'Someone help that goddamn horse!' he yelled hoarsely.

'Stay on the ground!' one of the cowboys yelled back.

At least half a dozen guns were pointing down at him. The stallion was still screaming. Then a bloodied figure staggered past the horsemen surrounding him. Zacchaeus stared up at the contorted face of Stewart Kerfoot. The man's hat was missing and dirt smeared his face. Blood poured from a cut in his head where the rifle butt had hit him.

'Damn you, sodbuster!' The youngster was hysterical with rage. 'You're gonna die for this!'

Stewart Kerfoot's hand was trembling as he held the gun pointed down at the fallen man. In the instant before the gun went off. Zacchaeus rolled forward and into the gunman's legs. With a wild scream the rancher went down.

Even as he fell Kerfoot was still trying to trigger the Colt. Zacchaeus grabbed the gun and pulled hard.

Stewart was yelling and cursing. There was a sudden flurry of movement around the struggling men as the horsemen hurriedly dismounted and piled into the fight.

The struggle was fast and vicious. An attacker reared back clutching a bloodied nose. Another screamed and rolled away in agony as a bony knee smashed into his groin. But there were just too many of them.

They used their gun butts and clubbed recklessly at the sodbuster as he savaged all who came within reach. As more and more blows rained down Zacchaeus's struggles became weaker and weaker.

He disappeared beneath a pile of wildly thrashing limbs and bodies. Even as he lay unconscious and helpless they kept up their attack as if fearful this ferocious man would suddenly spring to life and begin the struggle anew.

'Enough, enough!' someone was shouting. 'We got the sonovabitch!'

Slowly the frantic battering ceased.

Bit by bit the attackers disentangled from their victim. They were breathing hard, filled with anger and hatred for the man lying bruised and bloody in the dirt. Some vented their anger by kicking at the sodbuster. Their kicks brought no response from their victim. They glared down at him, cursing and swearing. His face, swollen and blood-ied, was almost unrecognizable.

They helped Stewart Kerfoot to his feet. His countenance was a mass of blood and dirt. There was something insane in the way his eyes stared out, wild and rolling. Sheriff Harrell pushed into the circle of men around the fallen Zacchaeus. He was just in time to see Kerfoot aim his gun at the inert figure on the ground.

'For Gawd's sake, Stewart!'

The lawman pushed the hand with the gun sideways. The gun fired but instead of hitting the fallen man in the head as intended, the bullet ploughed a bloody furrow along the side of his skull.

'What the goddamn hell you do that for, Sheriff?'

Stewart turned those mad staring eyes on the lawman. With anger twisting his face into an ugly mask he spun around and pointed the gun at the lawman.

'Stewart,' Harrell pleaded desperately, backing away from the maddened youngster. 'You can't just shoot the sonovabitch in cold blood. We gotta do this by the law.'

'The hell with the law,' the youngster raged, his face distorted with fury. 'This is Kerfoot law. We have our own kinda of justice for vermin.'

'Listen to me, Stewart. I don't wanna answer to your old man for something we can't fix. Arresting a man for assault is one thing but killing is something else again. We can still fix this sonovabitch and you'll get your revenge at the same time. We can get rid of him without any of us being held responsible. For God's sake listen to me. I know what I'm talking about.'

For long unsettling moments the youngster stared at the sheriff. The lawman was afraid his pleading had been in vain. Slowly the madness faded from the young Kerfoot's eyes. The gun he was pointing at the sheriff lowered.

'Talk, Sheriff, and it better be good. I want that sonovabitch dead and ain't no one stopping that from happening no matter what.'

The sheriff turned and yelled for someone to put that goddamn horse out of its misery. A gunshot rang out and the big stallion stopped squealing.

7

Before loading the body they examined him to establish if he was still alive. Sheriff Harrell knelt down and felt for a pulse. It took him some time to decide whether the man was alive or dead. The posse stood around staring curiously as the sheriff bent over and put his ear to the man's mouth.

'The goddamn sodbuster is still alive but only just. That head wound shoulda finished him. You can just about detect the heartbeat. By the time we get him into the hills he'll be buzzard meat.'

'Right, here's the plan. The fella told us he was going hunting. We transport him into the hills and leave him there. By the time he's found, if he ever is, he'll be eaten by wolves or coyotes or whatever the hell else wants a piece of him. There'll be so little left no one will be able to tell what he died of. Some of us takes him into the hills and leaves him. The rest go on to his place and ask around for him like we've still looking for him. That way we've covered our asses and no one will be any the wiser.'

'What about his horse? If that's found here there's no way he could have gone into those hills on foot.'

'Hell, you're right. We'll havta put a rope on it and drag it up there. Like the sodbuster it'll be well chewed afore anyone finds them. People will just assume he met with an accident.' The sheriff looked round sternly at the listening cowboys. 'After all this you keep your traps shut. We can't have no one blabbing about today's happenings. As far as anyone's concerned we came out here looking for the goddamn sodbuster and never caught up with him.'

They nodded in agreement. Then they went about their tasks in silence, somewhat subdued by what had happened. The effects of the liquor Stewart Kerfoot had plied them with was beginning to wear off.

'Another thing,' Stewart called. 'Every man here draws a bonus on his wages for today's work.'

This brought a few smiles and chuckles from the group. The cowboys went about their tasks with a renewed willingness.

Stewart Kerfoot headed for his mount. 'Sheriff Harrell, you organize the work. I'll ride over and ask around about Wolfe. I'll take some of my boys. We can go to the sodbuster's place. That should keep any suspicion from falling on us.'

Stewart waved a farewell and with a half a dozen of his cronies headed for the Wolfe homestead.

When they had attached the ropes to the stallion they laid slickers on the ground and dragged the carcass on to the waterproofs. Then they fastened these to the body of the stallion to protect it during the journey to the hills. It wasn't much but it was all they had to hand to make sure the carcass arrived in one piece without leaving too much of a trail. The injured sodbuster was much easier. Roughly they pushed him across a cowpony and tied him in place. When all was ready the posse set out. Two outriders rode wide to give warning of anyone that might chance to come their way and see what they were up to.

Sheriff Harrell supervised the preparations for the trip and at last pronounced himself satisfied they had done what they could to ensure the success of their mission.

'What the goddamn hell have I got myself into?' he muttered loud enough for some of the posse to overhear. The cowboys exchanged uneasy glances. 'Let's move out.'

The riders chosen as scouts galloped out into the plain in advance of the main body of horsemen. The men charged with the task of dragging the dead stallion tried to choose a path that had not too many snags. One man rode in front, warning of impending rocks or protruding roots that might cause a problem for the smooth passage of the slicker-wrapped carcass.

On grassland the body of the stallion slid along relatively smoothly. But it was hard going for the ponies roped to the dead horse. The animals did not like the thing they were dragging. Their riders had constantly to calm them and keep them pulling. As the party advanced it was agreed to spell the ponies and swap tasks from time to time.

When the party set out the distant foothills seemed far away. It was an uneasy group of cowboys that had the task of transporting their macabre burden. For the most part they progressed in silence. There was none of the banter cowboys usually indulged in.

The riders dragging the carcass of the big stallion were constantly looking over their shoulders to judge how their burden was standing up to the journey. They were fearful that the slickers would snag and rip. If that happened the hide of the stallion would begin to shred and tear and leave traces. They were anxious to get the carcass to the hills in as good condition as possible.

Once they dumped it they could depend on coyotes and wolves to rip and devour the animal. The same fate would befall the stubborn sonovabitch lying across a cowpony. When he was left in the hills the blood from his wounds would attract predators. In time there would be nothing left but a skull and a few scattered bones.

Their luck held and they encountered no one on the trip. They stopped once to change over the ponies dragging the big stallion. During the last part of the trip the slickers wrapped around the body of the stallion disintegrated. Quickly new pads were tied in place and the journey continued without further incident.

The group of horsemen pushed up through the foothills and into the tree-line. At last Sheriff Harrell held up a hand. The little party reined in their mounts and awaited instructions.

'Right, get those slickers off that there stallion.'

The cowboys jumped down to comply.

'What about this here sodbuster?'

'He look like he's coming round?'

'Naw, not a flicker of movement all the time we been riding. I reckon he's deader than a butchered steer.'

'In that case dump him off. Place him near the horse so if anyone happens to find him it'll look like he took a tumble and bust his head. With a bit of luck no one will discover them till after the coyotes have had a go.'

Inside the trees the posse set the scene. When they finished their gruesome work the man lay a few yards from the horse.

'What about that rifle of his?'

'Better leave that where it is. Remember he was on a hunting trip and took a tumble from his horse. The sooner we get away from this place the sooner the critters can get to work on him. The less we disturb the place the better.'

The posse clattered back down the slope leaving the horse and man as food for the various predators that inhabited the hills.

8

It was with some apprehension the woman observed the large body of horsemen as they rode across the plain. The riders looked of a type similar to the cowboys who had once before intruded into her life with such disastrous consequences. She retreated further up the hillside, watching and waiting. The large shaggy dog by her side sensed the riders and began growling.

'Hush, Cesario. We'll keep quiet and out of sight while we see what these varmints are up to.'

She put her hand down and laid it on the dog's head. It ceased to growl and obediently crouched beside her.

The woman was of indeterminate middle age. She had long grey hair tied back with a piece of rawhide. Her square craggy face might have been handsome when she was younger. Many seasons of wind and sun had sucked out any hint of youthfulness or soft lines from her features. A battered and stained old hat rested on her head. Her clothes were so patched and mended they made excellent camouflage. When she crouched behind a fallen tree and peered through the network of branches it was difficult to distinguish her against the dappled backdrop of the leaves.

Like a woodland satyr she watched unseen as the posse rode up into the woods. For a few unsettling moments she thought she would have to retreat further up the hill as the intruders pushed nearer and nearer her hiding-place. Then they came to a general halt. Up close now, she could see, the group was made up of cowboys. These were, without a doubt, her sworn enemies. Unconsciously she pushed her hand inside her patched and worn jacket and caressed the butt of the old Army Colt that nestled in the holster belted around her waist.

'Right, get those slickers off that stallion,' the big man in charge called.

She watched the cowboys as they went to work.

'What about the sodbuster?' a cowboy called out.

For the first time she saw the burden one of the cowponies was carrying. The sight of the blood-spattered man and the word *sodbuster* set off alarming memories.

The body was dumped to the dirt. She had no memory of drawing the weapon but the Colt was in her hand. It was taking all her self-control not to pull the trigger. Then she saw the badge. It was pinned on the coat of the man giving out orders to the cowboys. She tried to concentrate on what he was saying.

'With a bit of luck no one will find them till after the coyotes have had a go.'

'You bastard . . . ' the woman muttered.

There had not been much chatter from the men. They were almost finished now. Taciturn and restrained, their grisly work complete, the cowboys mounted. Wheeling their horses they filed silently from the trees. The woman kept her gun trained on the group till she was sure they were departing for good. She watched without moving from her hiding-place till the horsemen were vague shrinking figures in the distance.

'Cesario, foul murder has been committed or I'm no judge. A poor homesteader murdered and dumped up here to be eaten by the beasts. The killing must still be going on. My poor Raymond was only one of many to be murdered by the men of blood.'

She rested on her heels as the bad memories played once again in her head. Tears squeezed from beneath tight-shut eyes and trickled down her gnarled cheeks. The dog was looking dolefully at its mistress. Tentatively it reached out and began licking her hand. She opened her eyes and patted the dog's head.

'Sorry, Cesario, I thought I had gotten over that a long time ago. Some things never heal — like a broken heart. Don't you ever go giving all your love to one person. If anything happens to them it fair rips the heart outta one.' The sigh she emitted was long and soulful. 'Come on, I figure we can see if that fella had anything useful on him. Though it fair makes my flesh crawl to havta rob the dead. I guess it wouldn't go amiss to give the poor man a decent burial. I'll havta go back to the cabin to fetch the shovel.'

Again she sighed, then stood upright and made her way cautiously to the body lying motionless in the dirt. The dog followed obediently.

'I cain't touch the poor man just now. I'll have a look at the horse first. They left it fully saddled.'

Just then she stopped and stared out from the trees seeking for a sight of the horsemen. The posse was only a faint smudge far out towards the horizon.

'What if they come back to check on him?' She stood deep in thought. 'If'n they come back and see the bodies interfered with they may start looking for the one as did it.'

Thoughtfully she hung there, torn by indecision. And then she caught sight of the rifle stock protruding from the saddle bucket of the dead horse.

'Damn me, a rifle. To hell with the consequences, that rifle's mine.'

With a last look out over the prairie as if to reassure herself the band of killer cowboys was not riding back to the scene of the crime she bent down and tugged at the rifle stock. When it came free she stood holding it in both hands, admiring the weapon. Quickly she pulled out the loading mechanism and discovered a full magazine. Briefly a grim smile flickered across her face. She loaded the magazine, then put the rifle to her shoulder and pointed it in the general direction of the departing posse.

'Come back now, me boyos! Rose Perry is armed and ready to shoot herself a few skunks.'

She ached to try out her new acquisition but caution prevailed. A gunshot might just attract the attention she was anxious to avoid.

She rummaged through the saddle-bag, finding a packet of bread along with cheese and jerky and lastly a bag of coffee beans. All the while she was conscious of the dead body awaiting her attention. The companion to the first saddle-bag was trapped beneath the dead weight of the horse.

'I don't reckon I'll get to that. I might be able to cut the saddle girths and salvage the saddle anyway.' She stood up and turned slowly around to the task she had been putting off for as long as possible.

'Cesario! Dang your hide, dog! Get away from there!'

At the sound of her voice the dog looked up from the side of the lifeless man. It had been busy licking the dead face. The dog whined and wagged its tail.

'Shoo! You godamned mongrel!' she yelled, forgetting for the moment her own rules of stealthy and quiet behaviour while out and about.

Living in the hills she shared with the wild animals she had taught herself a code of wily woodcraft. She schooled herself to silence and slyness in all her activities. Furtiveness was essential to her survival in the wilds. The shock of seeing the dog by the corpse had shaken her out of her natural caution.

The dog was whining and wagging its tail, unwilling to leave the body. Reasserting control she pointed the rifle at the dog.

'Come away, you damned ghoul,' she hissed, 'or so help me I'll blow your goddamned head off.'

Instead of doing as it was told the dog crouched down again and laid his head on the man's chest. It kept whining and wagging its tail. An awful suspicion began to form in the woman's head.

'Cesario,' she whispered, 'what the hell you trying to tell me?'

She began to tremble so much she had to set the butt of the gun in the dirt and prop herself up by gripping the barrel. Slowly she shuffled forward using the rifle as a support. The dog kept up its pitiful whining and the tail redoubled its agitated wagging movement. For long moments she regarded the man.

'Damn my soul, I do believe this varmint's still alive!'

9

She had been working in the vegetable patch when they rode up. Now she stood by the fence leaning on the hoe. She tried staring out past them, knowing not to meet their eyes.

'My husband is not here at present. He went hunting. I'm surprised you didn't meet him on the road.'

The six horsemen sat their mounts eyeing up Gabrielle. Wolfe was such an insignificant man. Yet here he was living with this splendid woman he claimed as his wife.

She could feel the hostility in their gaze, or was there something more in their eyes than she could read?

'I guess we'll havta take a look,' Stewart Kerfoot said.

She said nothing, waiting patiently for them to go. 'He could be hiding in that there outhouse.'

She felt the dread in her heart, for she knew that peculiar expression in his eyes. It was a characteristic of ill-mannered men who lived by their passions. When men looked at her like that she had a way of withdrawing into herself, trying to make out she was invisible or untouchable. For a moment only she regretted sending Zacchaeus away. These rude men would not dare take such liberties if Zacchaeus Wolfe were at home. Immediately she quashed the thought. It was because she had known they would come looking for him she had sent him away.

Still, she was afraid: afraid for herself but most of all afraid for Zacchaeus. He was gone, safe in the hills for now. Still carrying the hoe, she came up to the front of the house and stood like a silent affront to all that they represented.

Stewart Kerfoot was a product of the wealth and power wielded by his family. The Kerfoots had come into this land when it was claimed by no one, only the

Indians. They had built their empire on the dead bodies of the savage Red Man. And because they had won that battle they were convinced they were invincible. The Kerfoots ruled this land and let no man or woman say different.

Stewart jumped down from his horse, handed the reins to Merrit Chase, then strutted across the yard. She felt his eyes on her as he approached.

'What right have you to come here on private property and harass innocent people. Is there no law in this country?'

'Law, ma'am! What law was your sodbuster husband obeying when he tried to murder me?'

For the first time she looked directly at him. She noted the bruised and swollen face, the fresh blood on the side of his head.

'If my husband was wanting to murder you, which I doubt very much, then you would not be here now bothering peaceful folk as want to lead a decent life.'

The youngster jabbed a finger at the bruises on his face.

'That sodbuster tried to murder me. Only my men come on the scene, or he would have succeeded. I tell you now I'm part of a posse sent out to apprehend that felon. If you want authorization for my actions just ask Sheriff Harrell. He's the one with the warrant for his arrest. We was deputized to search for him. Sheriff Harrell is out chasing around the country trying to find that sonovabitch. And when he does we'll throw him in jail and let him rot there. It's only what he deserves. So don't you try to interfere with the law or you might just end up in jail with that troublemaker husband of yours.'

Stewart turned and smirked at the men still sitting their horses and enjoying his performance.

'Sure thing, Stewart,' Steve Hewitt called out. 'Seems a pity for such a purty lady like this to spend her time rotting in jail. Say ma'am, how's about you could make us fellas a coffee? We can be real nice to a lady as purty as you.'

His companions were guffawing, getting excited by his suggestive talk. She gripped the handle of the hoe more tightly.

'Please leave now. Mr Wolfe is not at home. I am not sure when he will return. When he does I dare say he can answer to Sheriff Harrell for any of these alleged offences.'

'I sure am thirsty, ma'am. A mug of coffee would go down a treat. Chasing felons sure brings out a thirst in a fella.'

'Maybe she got a drop of homebrew stashed out in that there cabin.' Jason Lee joined in the banter. 'What do you say, fellas? What say we take a sashay in that there cabin and rest up a while from this here posse work?'

The cowboys were dismounting now.

'Damn good idea, fellas.'

Stewart came close to her, leering. She could smell the drink coming off him: alcohol and sweat and horsy smells and a body stench that was repulsive to her sensitive nose. She tried not to flinch from his closeness. He was grinning widely.

The rancher grabbed Gabrielle and pushed her towards the house. She could not help it. The action was instinctive. The hoe was in her hand. She drove the hickory handle into his face. It had not been her intention to hurt him.

The end of the handle drove into his mouth, mashing lips and jarring teeth. He screamed and stumbled back, blood pouring from his damaged mouth. Then rage engulfed him, overcoming the pain. He launched himself at Gabrielle, driving her back on the porch. Under his attack she stumbled and fell with Kerfoot on top.

'Damn blasted whore.'

He was screaming abuse as he battered her. She tried to fend him off with the hoe. It was useless at such close quarters. With a scream of rage he wrenched the implement from her grasp.

Kneeling on top of her he raised the hoe then drove it hard and brutally into her face. She cried out as the hardened wood broke her cheekbone. Again and again he smashed the hoe into Gabrielle's face. All the while he was screaming out his hate and his anger.

Ever since the encounter with Zacchaeus in town, when the sodbuster had so efficiently taken his gun away and smashed him to the boardwalk, the anger had been there. The capture and shooting of his enemy had dissipated some of that anger. Now this woman had had the temerity to hit him. It rekindled the savagery in him.

All reason left Kerfoot. Again and again he smashed the hoe into the face of the impudent woman. It was not Gabrielle's face he was hitting. It was the sodbuster who had humiliated him in front of his friends.

'Stewart! For gawd's sake, Stewart!' Merrit Chase jumped forward, making a grab for the maddened youngster.

The cowboys were grappling with

him, trying to pull him off the woman. He fought them, screaming and yelling.

'Goddamn bitch! Hit me, will she!'

They dragged him away. The woman lay unmoving.

'Jesus God!' George Rankin exclaimed. He turned and vomited into the dirt.

Stewart was still struggling against the men trying to restrain him.

'Let me go! I'll kill the bitch!'

'Boss, I don't think that'll be necessary.' Merrit Chase was breathlessly struggling with his young boss, trying to wrestle him away from the porch and the sight of the deed he had committed.

'She goddamn hit me, the filthy bitch! I'm gonna make her pay!'

He was almost foaming at the mouth, only it was blood he was spitting where the handle of the hoe had split his lips. Chase and Lee at last succeeded in dragging Stewart away from the porch.

There was no reasoning with the young range boss when he was in this mood. His men could only hold him and plead for him to cease his raging. The struggling men were over by the horses now, made skittish by the commotion.

Jacob Birch was kneeling on the porch examining the woman.

'Stewart, I think she's dead.'

10

It had taken all her ingenuity to get the wounded man moved. At first she had thought to build a shelter where he lay and tend him there. On reflection she did not consider that a wise arrangement.

'Them goddamn cowboys might just return. I heard tell a murderer allus returns to the scene of the crime. No, if I'm to make this fella safe then I havta move him.'

She gave the matter some thought. Cesario patiently sat by the wounded man as if there was a special bond between them. The dog rested his head on the man's chest and watched his mistress, following her with his eyes as she moved around.

First she examined the wound in his head. A deep gash had been gouged into the scalp along the man's head.

Blood had caked on the injury, sealing the wound for which she was grateful. Massive bruising extended from the line of hair and spread down into his face.

'Looks like a bullet creased his scalp. I guess for the moment I'll leave well enough alone. That blood has clotted on his head and the bleeding has stopped.'

Like all recluses she was in the habit of talking to the only other creature in her lonely life. The dog generally paid rapt attention to her patter and rarely answered back.

'Another half-inch and it would have opened his skull. As it is I ain't sure he'll ever recover from such an injury. Head wounds are funny things. It can leave a man half-paralysed or a drooling idiot. Whatever, it's my Christian duty to try and help the poor fella.'

Leaving the dog guarding the wounded man the woman returned to her refuge, an old abandoned line shack. The dog took its duties seriously and patiently sat by the man's side while his mistress was gone.

Dragging an old sled she used when foraging for firewood the woman duly returned. At one time she had constructed a harness for the dog so it could help drag the thing when laden. On the sled she had packed blankets and homemade bandages.

Carefully she bandaged the wound before attempting to move her patient. The injured man showed no signs of awareness or gave any other signs of life as he was rolled on to the primitive transport. The woman had to do this all the while taking care not to disturb the bandages she had used to bind the wound in his head.

'I sure as hell hope I ain't doing all this in vain,' she complained to the dog as she laboured.

It was a delicate and nerve-racking operation to get her patient on the sled. As she laboured over the task she was acutely conscious of the terrible head wound she was trying so earnestly not to make any worse. Somehow she managed to load her gruesome cargo and at last was able to harness Casario and begin the laborious task of rescuing the wounded man.

With her pulling on a rope attached to the sled and the dog straining on the harness it took her over an hour to get him to the cabin. Exhausted and with sore hands from hauling on the rope she almost collapsed when she reached the dilapidated shack she called home.

The patient showed no signs of returning life. Too exhausted to make the effort to bring him inside she decided to wrap him in blankets and hides and hope it did not rain. She knew the scent of blood would attract predators. Certainly the wounded man would be easy prey for any large animal that might come by in the night. But with Cesario standing guard she reasoned the dog would alert her to any danger.

'Well, boy, we just havta hope and

pray for the poor fella. Tomorrow I'll go out and cover up our tracks where we dragged that fella here. I'm too tired now to do anything other than have a bite to eat.' She stared down at the grey face of the wounded stranger. 'I reckon he ain't got a hope of a candle in hell of surviving, but at least we can say we done what we could.'

In the cold light of morning she thought her worst fears had come true. The face of wounded man seemed to have shrunk. The chiselled lines of his features had deepened to take on the aspect of a skull. At first glance the woman thought she was looking at the face of a corpse.

'It looks like the poor man has gone to the bosom of the Lord,' she said sorrowfully. 'All that work I done for him to die like that on me. I wonder who his folks are? I guess I'll havta poke about in his pockets and find if he has kin.'

She bent over the figure wrapped up in blankets and began to roll back the covers. For a moment she paused and frowned.

'I'll be danged, Cesario. I do believe this fella is clinging on to life.'

Plucking a long grey hair from her head she laid it across the man's nostrils. To her delight the hair fluttered in the weak flow of air from his lungs.

'There's nothing else for it; we gotta get this fella inside where I can keep an eye on him. If God so wills it he'll survive.'

Using the same method as she had the day before when she dragged the sled back to the dwelling, she managed to pull the weighty bundle up over the step and into the shack. Quickly she made up a bed of animal skins and dried grass on the floor and with some effort transferred her patient to a more comfortable resting place.

'I guess I'd better try and clean up that wound on your head. Maybe you're hardier than I think.'

Carefully she undid the bandage she had tied in place the day before. With a concerned expression she examined the injury.

'I'm gonna havta clean that there wound.'

Turning to a shelf upon which sat a row of small containers she selected a bottle that, according to the label, had once held whiskey. She poured a milky liquid into a dish of hot water. With considerable gentleness she spent some time cleansing the deep and ugly bullet wound in the man's head. The gash bled while she worked. The liquid in the bowl turned a deep pink. At last she set the cloth aside and studied the injury. She had to fasten a pad underneath the man's head for blood seeped constantly from the wound.

'I fear that wound is too deep,' she muttered. 'There's only one thing for it. I gotta sew it up. Otherwise it'll never heal.'

She fetched needle and thread and spent the next several minutes pulling the edges of the deep gash together and stitching a row of sutures along his scalp. When she finished her needle-work she sat back on her heels. Drops of sweat stood on her face. Critically she examined the result.

'Damn me, the poor fella won't recognize himself if he ever wakes up. Maybe his hair will grow over and cover it up. I sure hope I never have to do the like again.'

She took a small crock from the shelf of remedies and, using her finger, smeared a dark and pungent-smelling paste over the stitches.

'I guess that's the best I can do for the poor soul. It's in the Lord's hands now if he lives or dies.'

She gazed long and earnestly at the face of the man she was trying to save.

'I guess it wouldn't go amiss to give you a name, mister.'

She probed calloused fingers into his pockets. Her search yielded her no clue as to the man's identity. A sack of tobacco and matches, a clasp knife and a roll of string was all she found. She sighed deeply.

'I'll havta call you something. Can't just go on calling you mister.' She sat deep in thought. 'What about Raymond Daniels? My husband's name was Raymond Daniel Perry. I'm sure he won't mind none if'n you lend his name for a while till you wake up, if'n you ever do.'

'Right, Mr Raymond Daniels, sleep and heal. If you last another day I reckon you might just stay alive. Why you ain't dead now sure beats me.' She spent some time gently tucking the coverings around her patient. 'Mayhaps it's the Lord's will your time ain't up just yet. But my heart is sore afraid I'm keeping you alive to give you more grief when your senses return. Perhaps I should have left you there to die. I know a man as fell of'n his horse and split his head open. He became as an infant again and played with childish things. It was pitiful to see the children chase after him and call him names. His wife hanged herself in the end. Couldn't take the shame of it.'

After these reflections the woman took a well-worn old book and leafed through it for a time. At last she looked up and spoke to the man as if he were alert to her every word.

'I shall read to you from the Good Book, Mr Raymond Daniels. Jeremiah.'

For I will restore health unto thee, and I will heal thee of thy wounds, saith the Lord; because they called thee an Outcast, saying, This is Zion, whom no man seeketh after.

11

The posse rode up the main street of Consul, the riders tired and dispirited. Sheriff Harrell hauled up outside the jail and looked without surprise at the horses tied up outside.

'Looks like Kerfoot got the easy part of the hunt,' he remarked to no one in particular. 'He's back afore us.'

'Maybe he never went looking after all. Just came straight here.'

Some of the men sniggered. Without exception all were weary and depressed by the day's happenings. Things had started out well enough. Stewart Kerfoot had fed them liberal doses of whiskey. He had not stinted himself with the rotgut. As his men imbibed he talked of avenging the slur on the Kerfoot name. No sodbuster had ever laid a hand on a Kerfoot before. His pa had taught them goddamned sodbusters to respect him and, by God, Stewart Kerfoot would do the same.

Fired up with whiskey and Stewart's wild talk of revenge they had set out to teach the sodbuster a lesson. There had been no talk of anything more than bringing the man back to the town jail. The events of the day and the long ride back had sobered them up. Many were uneasy in their minds. They could not dismiss the thought that they were all complicit in a killing that amounted to mob justice.

Sheriff Harrell dismounted and after tying up his horse took his rifle from the scabbard and pushed inside his office. As he expected Stewart Kerfoot and his intimates were gathered inside waiting for him. Harrell said nothing but walked to the gun rack and put his rifle up. He unbuckled his gunbelt and hung that on a peg. Only then did he set down behind the desk and look directly at the men waiting for him.

The cowboys were lounging around

the room watching the lawman. He could tell nothing from their expressions.

'Well, it's done,' he said at last. 'That sodbuster is rotting out in those hills along with his horse. I can't see anyone ever finding him out there. I hope you all got your story right. We never saw the varmint. He was gone long afore we went out looking for him. Stewart, if your old man wants to post a reward I'll get a wanted poster printed out. That should clinch it.'

'Sheriff, this thing is worse than we imagined.'

The sheriff was rummaging inside a drawer. He looked up as Stewart Kerfoot spoke. He held up a blackened pipe, peered inside the bowl and frowned.

'Yeah, what's that?'

Harrell took out a thin blade and began cleaning out the pipe.

'When we got to the sodbuster's place we found his wife.'

The sheriff looked up at Stewart with

raised eyebrows and waited for him to continue.

'She was dead — murdered.'

Sheriff Harrell forgot his pipe and stared quizzically at the youngster, waiting for more.

'She was there in front of the shack lying with her head stove in. Horrible it was, blood all over the place. George Rankin sicked his guts up.'

The pipe was forgotten as the sheriff stared at the youngster.

'He killed his own wife! No wonder he wasn't gonna let us take him in. Damn me, this affair gets worser and worser. Well, that makes me feel a damn sight better. Not that his poor wife was killed but that the murdering sonovabitch got his just deserts.'

Stewart Kerfoot walked to the door.

'I'm taking the boys over to the saloon to buy them a drink. Sure need it after all we seen today. You can join us if you will.'

'Damn me, I think I will,' replied Harrell, shaking his head with a bemused expression on his face. 'Murdered his own wife. Makes you despair of human nature.'

The men filed out of the sheriff's office. The remainder of the posse were invited to join in the drinking session. They accepted with alacrity.

Soon the saloon was noisy with excited men. Members of the posse regaled the citizens of Consul with the gruesome tale of the callous sodbuster who tried to kill Stewart Kerfoot and then murdered his wife in a most brutal and foul manner. Stewart Kerfoot was the centre of attention as he told of how he had fought off the sodbuster's savage attack.

'Keep them drinks flowing,' he instructed the barkeep. 'My boys have earned a drink after chasing about all day looking for that goddamned sodbuster. I only wish I'da killed the murdering sonovabitch afore he went home and murdered his poor wife. It was just my good nature to allow him to go. It sure was a harrowing sight to see that poor woman. Her face all mashed in. There was blood everywhere.'

The more lies he told about the day's happenings and the more drink was consumed the more Stewart Kerfoot began to believe the tale he spun for his listeners.

'An' you never caught up with the murdering sonovabitch?'

'Nope, took off somewheres. My guess is he'll head north towards the Canadian border. Once he gets up there we'll never find him. He's a curly wolf all right. I'm gonna ask my pa to post a reward. A killer like that hasta be caught afore he kills again.'

'What sorta reward you got in mind, Stewart?'

Stewart drew his eyebrows down in concentration as he thought about the question.

'Hell, I know,' he said at last. Looking up he caught Sheriff Harrell's eye. 'What you think, Sheriff? How much to catch that killer?'

The sheriff was imbibing the free

drinks as fast as he could get the fiery liquor down his neck. Mostly he was drinking to blot out the day's events. He sank another shot before answering.

'I reckon we oughta ask your pa to post five hundred dollars. Yep, that should tempt the bounty hunters or anyone else as wants to go after that mean sonovabitch.'

'Five hunnert!' one of the drinkers exclaimed. 'That's damn near half a year's pay. What a fella couldn't do with five hunnert doesn't bear thinking about.'

'If I got my hands on that five hunnert, I'd have me a different gal every night of the week.'

'With a face like yourn, Harry, the gals would pay you not to bother them.'

It was a merry crowd gathered in the Elephant and Monkey getting drunk on Stewart Kerfoot's hospitality. Free drinks bought many a man's loyalty.

12

Richard Kerfoot harnessed up the buggy for the drive into Consul. Normally he would have taken a saddle horse but today he had come to a momentous decision about something. He put Barley, his pet mare, between the shafts.

'You'll like Miss Lavinia, Barley,' he assured the horse.

Ever since meeting the dressmaker that day with his mother he had been unable to get the girl out of his mind. His mother's disparaging remarks about Lavinia had made no difference to his feelings. The girl had set fire to his imagination and since the meeting he had been unable to dismiss her from his thoughts. Now he was taking the first step towards getting to know the dressmaker better.

Good day, Miss Lavinia. I was in town on an errand and I hope you don't mind me calling to say, howdy.

The more he rehearsed the greeting the more nervous he became. He had seen her with her little notebook answering his mother and now he imagined her writing a reply to him.

Mr Kerfoot, how lovely. Would you care to take tea with me?

Yes Miss, that would sure be a pleasure but first how about a little jaunt out in my buggy?

Indeed it is a lovely day for a ride. Just let me fetch my bonnet.

See here, this is Barley, one of my thoroughbred mares. She steps out real pretty. See how she holds her head so proud and how delicately she jogs in the harness.

Oh, Mr Kerfoot I've never seen anything so beautiful.

I wanted to make a present of this outfit to you, Miss Lavinia.

At this stage in the fantasy the girl throws her arms around him. They don't speak, just stand there holding each other.

The town loomed ahead. The young man came back to reality with a start. The nervous tension was building in him. He started sweating.

'It's no good,' he muttered. 'She'll just smile politely and tell me she does not accept gifts from strange men.'

The mare trotted on oblivious to her master's growing agitation. They come to the town boundary. Richard began to regret the impulse that had sent him into Consul on a fool's errand. He reined in the mare and slowed the animal down to a walk. At a snail's pace the buggy entered the main street of the town.

Richard Kerfoot did not register details of the stores and offices lining the street. The false-fronted stores held no interest for him except for one. All too soon the Parisian scene above the dressmaker's store loomed in sight. For a moment he panicked and almost drove past. His hands jerked on the reins and the mare, as if intent upon thwarting her master, hauled to a stop in front of Lavinia's Fashions. There was nothing else for it. Richard had to alight. For a moment he fussed with the harness, then reluctantly tied up. Wiping his sweaty palms on the seat of his pants he pushed on into the shop.

The little bell on the spring tinkled mockingly. There was no one in attendance in the shop. Richard stood undecided, sweating some more and waiting for someone to respond to the bell. The minutes ticked by and no one appeared. Idly he looked around him at the shelves filled with rolls of coloured cloth. Hats and gloves were displayed on shelves at varying heights. At several vantage points there stood mannequins adorned in lady's attire. The place smelled of fabric and hot smoothing irons. Thinking to attract some notice Richard coughed loudly. He immediately regretted making such a noise in the stillness that enclosed him in the store.

At last he decided to retreat. It was a cowardly decision but one that was understandable. He was in the act of turning towards the door when a slight noise brought him around again. The young black woman came through the curtains and into the store. There was a distracted look about her as she walked towards the counter, apparently without noticing the man standing in the shop.

'Ahem.' Stewart cleared his throat.

Her head swung round with the look of a startled deer. She was an attractive-looking girl with somewhat chubby features. Her eyes looked swollen as if she had been weeping.

'Lord almighty, I didn't see anybody there. We're closed, sir. If you care to come back another day we can see to your needs.'

'It's Miss Lavinia I come to see.'

She frowned as she examined him, as if trying to recall where she had seen him before.

'You're Mrs Kerfoot's boy. Is it about the dress she collected?'

'No, miss, it . . . well . . . it's a personal matter I wanted to see Miss Lavinia about.'

Before she could reply Lavinia emerged from the back of the shop. She stared silently at Richard. To his consternation Miss Lavinia's eyes looked red and puffy as if she too had been weeping.

'I . . . is anything the matter, Miss Lavinia? Is there some sort of trouble?'

'Please, Mr Kerfoot, now is not a good time.' The black girl moved towards Richard. 'We're just on our way out.'

'My buggy is outside. Perhaps I could drive you wherever you want to go.'

The women exchanged glances. Richard caught the slight shake of Lavinia's head.

'Thank you, Mr Kerfoot, we already have transport. Now if you don't mind we need to lock up and be on our way.'

She was walking towards him. Politely but firmly she ushered him towards the door.

'Miss Lavinia,' Richard tried once more, 'there's a perfectly good buggy outside. I insist you let me drive you and your assistant to wherever you want to go.'

'Mr Kerfoot, please leave now. We have no need of you or your rig. Your family has caused enough grief as it is.'

She was pushing him gently but firmly to the door. He stared over the head of the young black woman. Lavinia was looking intently back at him, her eyes dark pools of anguish. He observed her anxiously chewing on her lower lip. Her companion placed the flat of her hands against his chest and was gently but firmly pushing him to the exit.

'No, wait,' he said, suddenly bracing himself against the pressure on his chest. 'Miss, I sure don't know what is going on but I came here today to offer you a gift of that there buggy tied up outside your store. I . . . I just wanted to get to know you better.'

He stumbled to a halt and stared helplessly at the young woman. She turned abruptly and walked back through the curtains. He stared helplessly after her.

The pressure on his chest from the young black woman became insistent. He felt himself being pushed back out on to the boardwalk. The door was firmly closed in his face.

'Goddamn it, what the hell's the matter with those females? What did I say?' Richard slapped his hat against his leg and stared with mounting frustration at the closed door. 'Damnit, I need a drink.'

He grabbed the reins of his buggy and dragged the mare around to face back down the street. It was only a few hundred yards to the saloon. Richard tied up and stomped inside.

'Whiskey.'

The barkeep knew all the Kerfoot family. He seldom saw this one inside his bar. Having poured a measure, he was moving away when the youngster stopped him.

'Leave the goddamn bottle.'

'Sure.'

It was early in the day and the place was almost empty. Mindful of the importance of the Kerfoots in the community the barkeep decided it would do no harm to be convivial towards this youngster.

'How's that brother of yours, Stewart? He healed up yet?'

Richard looked up. He was in no mood for idle conversation but innate good manners compelled him to be polite.

'Yeah, I reckon so.'

Richard remembered the cuts and bruises on his brother's face and his black eyes. He had come home covered in blood but claimed it was chicken blood. Stewart was always getting into brawls and Richard, preoccupied with his own feelings, had not taken much notice of his brother's injuries. The barkeep folded his arms and leaned forward.

'What you reckon about that sodbuster and him having a fight?'

Richard stared back, shaking his head.

'According to your brother the

sodbuster attacks him but Stewart's men pulled them apart. The sodbuster then goes back home in a mad rage and murders his own goddamn wife. Stewart wants the sheriff to arrest the man for attacking him. The posse goes out to the sodbuster's place and finds the wife with her face all bashed in and no sign of the husband. Dreadful thing.' The barkeep shaking his head with his lips pursed. 'Terrible. They burying the poor woman this morning.'

Richard was staring at his informant. He was remembering the two women at the dress shop. They were wearing black clothes as if in mourning or preparing to go to a funeral, their eyes red and weepy.

'Jesus wept!' Leaving his drink untouched Richard Kerfoot turned and hurriedly left the saloon.

13

It had been three days since the woman had rescued the wounded man. Each day she patiently spooned broth and herbal medicines into that slack mouth, spilling some but watching the man's convulsive swallowing as a little of the liquid went down. On the third day she approached her patient and stopped short. His eyes were open and he was watching her.

'Howdy,' she said gently, her heart beating fast as she regarded him.

'Where am I?'

The man spoke in a low but clear voice. She noted there was no slurring of his words.

'This is my home. It was an old line shack as I took over.'

'My head feels bad. I hear people talk about a splitting headache. Now I sorta know what that means.'

He reached up and gingerly probed the wound she had stitched together. Gently he traced his fingers along the injury, then took away his hand and looked at the residue of ointment transferred to his fingers. He examined the fingers for a moment before looking up at her.

'You do all this?'

She nodded. 'How do you feel?'

'I feel as if someone split my head open with an axe and left the axe blade in there.'

She held up a bowl. 'I made some broth. It's got herbs in as might help. I been feeding it to you since I found you.'

He regarded her steadily. She noted his eyes were clear, as was his speech.

'What happened to me?'

'You . . . you don't remember?'

He went to shake his head and stopped. His eyes closed and spasms of pain and something else flickered across his face.

'I reckon you were shot. The bullet

ploughed a furrow along your scalp as wide as a railroad track. I had to sew it together. Head wounds can be funny things. I was a mite worried you would wake up an idiot. I was afraid the injury might have damaged your brain. Perhaps I should introduce myself. My name is Rose Perry. How are you called?'

His eyes opened. He looked back at her. 'I can't recall.'

She nodded sagely. 'It'll take a while but it'll all come back to you.' She held up the bowl. 'Do you feel able to take this broth afore it goes cold?'

'I'll try.'

She assisted him to a more upright position. Sweat was pouring down his face. He closed his eyes and sat silent. She waited patiently. Eventually he opened his eyes again and reached for the bowl.

'You want me to spoon it?'

He kept his hand out without replying. She passed him the bowl and watched as he wedged the bowl between his body and the forearm of his handless limb. He began to spoon the liquor to his mouth. He took his time. The spoon was held steady and nothing spilled.

'You were going to tell me what happened,' he asked suddenly.

'You was dragged here by a gang of cowboys. For some reason they dragged your dead hoss along with you. They left you and the hoss and rode off. I suspect they was the ones as shot you. I reckon they thought you were dead. For some reason they didn't want anyone to find your body. You say you don't recall any of this?'

He closed his eyes. 'Nothing. I remember nothing, not my name nor how I came to be here.'

'While I was waiting for you to wake up I gave you a name. I would talk to you. I heard tell when someone has a bad injury talking to them can help. Maybe until your memory comes back you can use that name. I read you passages from the Good Book.'

He regarded her steadily.

'My late husband, rest his soul, was called Raymond Daniel Perry. I been calling you Raymond Daniels and I'm Rose.'

'Raymond Daniels,' he tried out the name. 'That's good enough for me, Rose. Can you tell me more about the men you say brought me here?'

'Mostly cowboys; I reckon from the Lazy K ranch. That's the biggest spread around here. In fact it's about the only spread.' Her eyes narrowed. 'There was one thing. There was a lawman with them there critters. He was telling them what to do. You in trouble with the law? Not that it makes any difference to me. I'd still 'a looked after you.'

'Rose, I can't remember anything. If you say it was cowboys maybe I was rustling cattle and they caught me. Makes sense to shoot me and dump the body. Lots of places they hang rustlers outright. You said something about them bringing along my dead horse. What was that all about?'

'Raymond, perhaps I should call you Ray. How does Ray Daniels sound?'

'Sounds fine to me, Rose. Tell me about the horse.'

'There ain't nothing to tell. I was out hunting with Cesario, my dog, when I saw the riders. I hid and watched them. They had ropes attached to the hoss and had dragged it with them. Fine-looking hoss too.' She paused and frowned. 'You wouldn't 'a stolen that hoss? It looked a mighty fine beast even lying there dead. Maybe that's what all this is all about.'

'Anyway, I waited till they all ride away and went to have a look. I thought you were dead so I went to the hoss first to see if I could find anything of value. There was a good rifle and some food in the saddle-bag. I brought that back with me.' When she finished speaking she noticed his eyes were closed. 'You still with me, Ray?'

His eyes opened and he looked steadily at her. Just then there came a scratching at the door and a dog began whining.

'That'll be Cesario. He been out having a ramble. Seems to 'a taken a liking to you. Mostly he sits by your bed and waits for you to wake up.'

'You better let him in then.'

There came a sharp yelp from outside.

'He hears your voice. Guess he wants to come in and say howdy.'

Cesario bounded through the door and ran excitedly to the injured man's pallet. The tail was wagging so hard it was a wonder the dog's back end didn't take off. The man put his hand out, the dog snuffled and licked it and got even more excited.

'Cesario, sit!' Rose commanded.

The dog obediently sat but it didn't stop its tail from wagging.

'Damn fool dog. You'd think you was his long lost brother come home from the wars.' She paused a moment after this comment and watched her patient continue spooning his soup. 'Talking about wars, was that how you lost your hand?'

Before replying he handed her the empty bowl. Solemnly he regarded the stump where his hand should have been. Something stirred in the back of his mind. He tried to focus on that but the moment vanished.

As she watched his face at first she thought he was not going to answer. He laid his head back against the pillow.

'For the life of me I can't remember. Until you said I hadn't even noticed I had a hand missing.'

His eyes were closed and he seemed to be asleep. Rose left him lying there with the dog stretched out by his pallet.

14

Richard drove the buggy out to the cemetery. As he drew near the burial place he could see people standing beside the vehicles drawn up at the entrance.

'I just hope I'm still in time.'

Heads turned towards him as he approached. He could see the two women and what he thought was preacher standing beside the gates. As he drew nearer he could hear someone singing in a raucous, drunken voice.

'Run boys run
The Yankees have come
Johnnie run and Johnnie flew
Johnnie tore his uniform in two
Run boys run
The Yankees have come.'

'What the hell's going on? This ain't

like no funeral I ever been to,' he muttered. 'Whoa there, whoa!'

The horse obediently stopped. As Richard wrapped the reins around the brake handle he was eyeing up the two vehicles already parked. One was a smart buggy he assumed belonged to the preacher. And the second was an open wagon in which was placed a pine coffin. Richard doffed his hat as he approached.

'Howdy, Reverend.' The preacher nodded back. 'Miss, I come to offer my apology for bursting in on your grief today. I wasn't aware of your bereavement.'

As Richard stood and made his apologies the drunken singing continued. There was no sign of the singer. Richard frowned and peered past the funeral party. For the first time he could see someone sitting inside the graveyard resting against the fence. A pair of muddy boots stretched out on the dirt. He assumed they belonged to the singer.

The song was in full swing. Richard had heard the song before. It was a Federal song about the war with Johnnie Reb running from the Yankees. While the Confederate soldier ran he threw away his weapons and his clothes and ended up running naked through briers and receiving injuries in various unmentionable parts of his anatomy.

'What's going on?'

'It's that vile wretch, Clive Perkins,' the preacher answered testily. 'These ladies made the mistake of paying him before he had completed his duties. Now we have a half-dug grave and a drunken gravedigger and no one to help with the coffin.'

Lavinia was looking attentively at him with stricken eyes. Richard ached to reach out and comfort her. She looked away.

'Maybe I could help out.'

He stuck his hat back on, walked past the preacher and moved up to stare down at the drunken gravedigger. The singing stopped.

113

'Howdy, fella, have a snort.' The man held out a jug invitingly. 'Clive Perkins was never one to deny a fella a drink when he needed one. Is thirsty work digging holes for planting dead folk.'

The man cackled loudly and returned the neck of the jug to his lips. He sucked noisily and liquid gurgled into his mouth. When he had swigged enough he placed the jug on his lap and began to cackle loudly.

'Yous come for the blackberrying, boy?' the drunken man chirruped and continued to guffaw.

'This is intolerable. Miss Wolfe, I can't hang around here any longer. You'll have to postpone the funeral till a later day.'

The preacher turned towards his buggy with the obvious intention of heading back to town.

'Hang on there, Reverend,' Richard intervened. 'I'll dig the grave and help with the funeral if that's permissible.'

The preacher hesitated, torn between duty and the necessity to bring this embarrassing situation to a close. In the meantime Clive had started up his Confederate song again.

'With your permission, miss?' Richard pleaded.

For a moment the two young people stared into each other's eyes. He saw pain mixed with shyness and waited patiently for her to make some sign that she would welcome his help.

Lavinia was intrigued by the determination of the young man in his resolve to help. His forthright manner and persistence reminded her somewhat of her Uncle Zac.

Since losing the power of speech in a horrific attack[1] she had successfully avoided the attention of the opposite sex by the simple expedient of never placing herself in their company. The dressmaking shop was an ideal location to hide from the male population, seeing as the clientele were all women.

---

[1] See, *Zacchaeus Wolfe*, Robert Hale, 2007.

Now this young man was pushing himself forward and intruding into her private world.

Distraught by the terrible events of the past couple of days she was a haze of conflicting emotions. Confused and flustered she could only nod her acquiescence to Richard to signal her acceptance of his help.

'Thank you, Master Kerfoot,' Lavinia's young black companion spoke up in place of Lavinia. 'I don't think we have been properly introduced. My name is Angelina Gobden and this is Lavinia Wolfe.'

Richard touched the brim of his hat. 'Thank you, Miss Angelina, Miss Lavinia, I sure am sorry for your trouble. I'll do what I can.'

Richard stepped inside the cemetery. Clive was still singing his bawdy song. Richard bent down and wrenched the jug from the drunk's slack hand.

'What the hell you doing, you young fool? That's my hooch, bought and paid for.'

'Listen, you old reprobate. You hush your foul mouth up while this burial takes place with or without your help.' Richard shook the jug and estimated at least half its contents had been consumed. 'I'm confiscating this here jug till this burial is over. If you behave yourself and keep quiet while it is taking place then I'll return the jug to you afore we leave. If you don't behave and keep quiet then I'll pour this here rotgut into the dirt.' To emphasize his threat Richard tipped the jug and a small stream of liquor poured from the neck.

'No . . . please, young'un . . . gimme the jug. I'll behave.'

'When the burial is done,' Richard said firmly.

He turned and walked into the cemetery. The unfinished grave was not hard to spot. A shovel was planted in a pile of dirt partway inside the grave-yard. Behind him Clive muttered dire predictions of death for the youngster if he didn't return the whiskey.

Richard ignored the threats. He set the jug beside the partially dug grave. Then he seized the shovel, jumped into the hole and began to dig energetically. The women and the preacher gathered round to observe his progress.

The knowledge that Lavinia was watching gave the youngster added energy. Under her watching eye he felt he could have dug up most of the prairie. The dirt fairly flew up from the hole. From time to time he paused to wipe away the sweat that poured in rivulets from his brow.

At one stage he paused in his digging and glanced up at Lavinia. Once again their eyes met and Richard felt that ache of yearning for this lovely young woman. Lavinia quickly dropped her eyes from his, but he was content. For a brief moment he had caught something in her eyes he dared to think was more than mere gratitude for his efforts to aid her in her distress. He redoubled his labours and relished the chance to show off his strength.

'Young man, I think that's deep enough,' the preacher called to him.

Richard stopped his digging and looked up at the figures standing looking down at him. His shoulders were now level with their feet.

'Sure, Reverend.'

Richard tossed out the shovel. With a quick heave he pulled himself from the grave. He stood and nodded to the young women. Lavinia was looking at him with some concern. Suddenly she stepped forward and, removing a small scarf from around her neck, she began to dab at his face. Her own face showed some disquiet.

For a moment Richard felt light-headed. The nearness of the young woman and her concern for his welfare was a heady mixture. That she was wiping the sweat from him was a truly tender moment for him.

He stood perfectly still while she worked on him, unwilling to move in case he broke the spell. The flawless features so near and the delicate hand earnestly dabbing his face were acting like a drug upon him. Her perfume permeated all his senses. It was a soft and subtle fragrance. He breathed in, gently absorbing the delicate scent. So rapt was he in these pleasurable sensations at that moment he was incapable of movement.

15

'Ahem. Young man, we still have to bring the coffin in.'

Richard was in such a daze he hardly registered the preacher's words. He did not want this intimate moment with Lavinia to end. The preacher had to repeat his request.

'I . . . ah . . . ' Richard reluctantly gave his attention to the preacher. 'Sir . . . ?'

Lavinia stepped back and dropped her eyes. Her face went bright red as she realized what she had done. She was unable to account for the impulse that had prompted her to step forward and wipe at the sweat on Richard's face. His strength and vitality and willingness to help drew her like a magnet. Somehow, when he vaulted from the grave he had looked so young and vital and powerfully attractive she was all of a sudden stirred out of her usual reserve.

When Richard had sufficiently composed himself he headed for the entrance where the cart holding the coffin stood. The gravedigger was silent and at first Richard believed the man was obeying his admonitions to be quiet. Then he saw the man was asleep. His head lolled to one side and he was snoring gently.

'Goddamn whoreson won't be able to help,' he muttered irreverently.

Quickly he lowered the tailgate. Taking a grip on the coffin he began to drag it towards him. Almost immediately he stopped. He turned as the preacher and the girls approached.

'It's mighty heavy. Even with all four of us helping I don't think we'll manage. Maybe I should go back in town and fetch some help?'

The preacher was becoming more and more irate.

'This is intolerable! That man should be publicly whipped.'

Before anyone could reply to this judgement the rumble of vehicles could be heard. They turned and watched as a convoy of carts, buggies and horsemen approached.

'What's going on, Reverend?' Richard asked. 'Is that another funeral arriving?'

'Not to my knowledge, but it might just be our salvation.'

The party arrived and drew up in a cloud of dust. Rough men in homespun clothes were alighting. They were dirt farmers and nesters, or sodbusters in the lingo of the cowhand who considered them an inferior breed. A big bluff man with extensive sideboards and a long, hooked nose approached. With hat in hand he nodded to the preacher.

'Thank the Lord we are in time.' He turned to Lavinia. 'We came as soon as we heard the news, miss. My name is Adrian Launder. I come to pay my respects to Gabrielle. I guess you must be Miss Lavinia, Zacchaeus's niece. He was real proud of you seeing as you were making a good business in town. This is a terrible business. It don't make no sense. Zacchaeus Wolfe was a good friend to anyone as needed help. Now we hear Gabrielle is dead an' Zacchaeus in on the run.' He shook his head. 'It ain't right. Gabrielle will be sorely missed. She had a great gift of healing and there's many a one here today can testify to her willingness to aid the sick and anyone else as needed her.'

Lavinia nodded her head and smiled wanly at the stranger. By now the party had disembarked and were gathered beside the cart with the coffin.

'We were just about to carry the coffin into the graveyard,' the preacher told the assembled crowd. 'We are a mite short of pall-bearers. If some of you would like to volunteer we can get this poor soul interred.'

'That's what we come for, Reverend.'

There was a general clatter of voices and men moved forward. Adrian Launder took charge, insisting on shouldering one corner of the coffin while three of his neighbours took the remaining positions.

Richard would have liked to be a pall-bearer but the newcomers were sidelining him. Angelina saw his predicament. She came over to him and whispered.

'Master Kerfoot, would you escort Lavinia and myself to the graveside?'

Richard nodded, grateful to be included. The little procession filed into the cemetery and made its way to the newly dug grave. The preacher took over.

'Dear friends and family, we have gathered here together in order to inter our sister Gabrielle, cut down in the prime of her life.'

After the service the mourners came one by one to Lavinia, murmuring condolences. Angelina held up her hand to get their attention.

'As some of you may know, Miss Lavinia, due to an unfortunate accident when she was younger, is unable to speak. But on her behalf I must thank you all for this kind and Christian deed today. We would be much obliged if you would come back to Consul with us and partake of some refreshments.'

'Miss, it sure is kindly of you to invite us but it would be like inviting a swarm of locusts into your home. These men would eat you out of house and home and then start on the house.' There was a general murmur of subdued laughter at this. 'However much we would like to dally, while we are here our farms are lying unprotected. There's been a lot of trouble for us smallholders. Cattle driven into crops, shots fired into houses. We came today to pay our respects to a good neighbour. No matter what anyone says, Zacchaeus Wolfe did not murder his wife. If you ask me those murdering cowboy scum at the Lazy K have a hand in this dirty work.'

'Hold on there, fella.' Richard stepped forward. 'That's a helluva accusation to make. There are no murderers working at the Lazy K.'

'Just who might you be young fella?'

'I'm Richard Kerfoot. My pa owns the Lazy K.'

There was a sudden shifting of people and a low murmur from the crowd of men behind Adrian Launder.

'Kerfoot, by God!' Suddenly the farmer seemed mindful of the women standing by the grave. 'Mr Kerfoot, this is not the time nor place to argue with you. When you return home tonight to the Lazy K ask your father how his cattle are driven so regular to trample our crops and break our fences. Why at night shots are fired at our houses and fires get started when we are away from home, like now, perhaps?'

Abruptly Adrian Launder turned and walked away. His companions stared with anger and hostility at Richard, then they too followed their leader's example and left.

Helplessly the youngster turned and looked at Lavinia who stood with bowed head. The preacher touched her shoulder, spoke softly to her, nodded to

Richard and left also. The jingle of harness and the rumble of wheels were heard as the farmers drove away. In a short time only Lavinia, Angelina and Richard remained.

'Master Kerfoot, Miss Lavinia and myself are grateful to you for all your help. We would be obliged if you would come back to the house for some refreshments.'

'That sure would be an honour, Miss Angelina, and I would be obliged if you would call me Richard.'

16

Rose heard the noise and looked round in some alarm. She had been dozing in her rocker. When she opened her eyes her patient was standing upright. His face was deadly pale and he was swaying slightly.

'Lord 'a mercy, what are you doing?'

'I could do with a stick or something to hold on to.'

'A stick! Your shouldn't even be on your feet!' She was out of the chair now and gazing at him with some concern.

'Rose, I can't just lie there and let you take care of me. I owe you my life as it is.'

'Men! They're stubborn as mules an' then some,' the woman grumbled as she stumped over and handed Zacchaeus a broom.

Cesario was excitedly running round in tight circles threatening to upset the man as he shuffled towards the door.

'You going outside?'

'I can't stand being cooped up like this. I need fresh air.'

She obediently opened the door for him. He gave her a tight grin and manoeuvred out on to the rickety porch.

After that painfully slow start he made rapid progress. With each excursion he went further and further. In time he dispensed with the broom.

'You remembering anything more?' she asked him.

'There's vague shadows in the back of my mind.' he said. 'There's a female appears from time to time. I see her face and she begins to speak, then just fades.' His brow furrowed as he concentrated. 'Then another female takes her place. Her mouth opens as if she wants to speak but no sound comes out. When I sleep, I dream of war. There is much bloodshed.' He raised his arm and stared at the stump. 'I have two hands in the dreams.'

She was silent as he pondered his lost life.

'Take me to the place you found me.'

She marvelled at his recuperative powers as they made the short trip. He crouched down beside the rotting carcass of the stallion. Reaching out he touched the hide, waiting quietly as if this link with the past would somehow jolt his memory.

'It was a noble beast.'

He walked around the carcass, pausing at the broken leg bones and crouching down to examine the injury. He raised his bearded face to look at her. There was no shaving equipment in the shack. He had been clean-shaven when she rescued him but now the fur on his face was thickening. The growth was streaked with grey. The beard suited his gaunt face and gave him a certain grand dignity.

'The horse's leg was broke which was why they had to drag it. But why wouldn't they let it lie where it fell. The buzzards and coyotes have it half-ate already.' He stood for a long time gazing out over the prairie, deep in thought. 'Rose, I gotta go out there and try and find out what happened.'

'We ain't got no horse and you'll never make it walking in your state. Anyway, you might be in trouble if'n you go back. Them as dumped you here sure didn't want you to survive.'

'I can't live without knowing.'

'I thought you'd say that. Every couple of months a friend of mine drives a wagon out here with supplies for me. We can ask him if he'll give you a lift to where you wanna go. He might even know who you are.'

'When's this friend of yours due?'

'Oh, I figure he's about due in a week's time. You'll havta take it easy till then. Mebby rest up a mite and recover your strength.'

'I might at that.' He eyed the dead horse. 'That's a mighty good saddle on that beast.' He knelt down and began to unbuckle the rig. 'The only thing is to figure out how to move this carcass to recover the darn thing.' He studied the lie of the ground. 'I reckon if I can fasten a rope around the neck I can tug that beast down this slope and free it from the saddle. With me pulling on the horse and you hanging on the saddle we should move it enough to drag it free. Tomorrow, I'll make a start on it. You say you found a rifle in the scabbard?'

'Yep. It was too good a find to leave lying there.'

'Why didn't the folk as did all this not take the rifle? The horse was dead; they must have thought I was dead too, so they dump us both here. Why didn't they take the rifle?' He was still squatting down where he had begun to loosen the harness from the dead horse. For a long moment he was quiet. 'If I came upon a horse with a broken leg and a dead man with a head injury I'd like as not think it was an accident. The horse broke a leg and threw the rider. He cracks his head open and lies there helpless. Along come the buzzards and the coyotes and tear the bodies apart. When that happens it'll be even harder to figure it out.' Slowly he straightened up. 'You say a lawman was giving orders. Something stinks here and I'm not talking about this rotting carcass.'

'Rose, when we get back to the shack I want you to describe everything you remember about that body of horsemen as dumped me here. Especially that lawman. And dig that rifle out.'

Zacchaeus Wolfe, known to both himself and Rose Perry as Ray Daniels, stared thoughtfully out across the plain beyond. Rose was watching him and at that moment caught something in his eye that sent a shiver up her spine. She watched as he ambled down the slope and leaned against a tree trunk.

'What have I resurrected?' she muttered. 'Perhaps those cowboys had good reason to want my lodger dead.'

17

'What the hell you mean, you insolent puppy!' Barrett Kerfoot stared with anger-reddened face at his youngest son. 'Since when did the affairs of sodbusters become your business?'

Richard stared back stubbornly. 'I only asked the question. A man called Adrian Launder asked the same questions of me yesterday when I attended the funeral of a nester's wife.'

The look on Kerfoot senior's face took on a deeper hue of red. 'You attended the funeral of a sodbuster! What the hell have I raised here!' Barrett darted a glance at Martha Kerfoot, standing by the fireplace anxiously watching the confrontation between father and son. 'Some saddle tramp stray into my bed while I was away on a cattle drive?'

Martha Kerfoot's lips tightened. She

knew better than to retaliate to her husband's jibes. Barrett was a burly man who over the years had packed fat on his big frame. He had a blunt and beefy face to match his powerfully built body. She had heard him make the same insults in the past and knew enough of his violent temper to turn the other cheek.

She was watching her son and stared fascinated as his face slowly reddened with rage.

'Take that back,' he gritted out. 'Ain't no one call my ma what you just said.'

Martha Kerfoot knew she should intervene now before this confrontation got out of hand. She could see all the danger signals. Her husband was a powder keg and Richard was the spark about to set it off. But Martha was mortally afraid of her husband. She watched helplessly and prayed inwardly.

Richard was standing before his father and in spite of his own muscular build looked slender before his father's bulk. His fists were clenched and he stood defiantly staring at his father.

Barrett Kerfoot frowned angrily. 'I say what I want in my own house. Now you get on your knees and apologize for being so sassy. Else I'll take a whip to you. Don't you think you're too old to feel the back of my hand! I'll have respect in my own home.'

'I ain't saying sorry for nothing till you apologize to Ma for that slur on her good name.'

Barrett Kerfoot's hand whipped out. It was as unexpected as it was sudden. He backhanded his son across the face. So powerful was the blow the youngster staggered back, blood pouring from a busted lip. Martha gasped and her hand covered her mouth as she watched helpless and scared.

Richard recovered his balance and stared balefully at his father. Slowly he touched his lip and looked at his bloody fingers. His father towered over him, a scowl on his face.

'Now say you're sorry,' he growled, 'afore your mouth is too busted to talk.'

'Is this how you answer awkward questions? You don't tell lies about nothing; you just beat down the opposition. Those sodbusters are trying to wring out a meagre living on the margins of your property. They have little or nothing and you do your best to make things even harder for them. You order our men to drive our cattle into their crops. You break down their fences; you fire barns and shoot into their houses — '

The tirade was cut off as Barrett Kerfoot smashed a fist into his son's face. Richard went down with a crash. There was a strangled scream from Martha. Stubbornly the youngster climbed to his feet.

'That's a compelling argument, Pa! Brute force in the face of any criticism.'

Again the senior Kerfoot lashed out. This time his meaty fist hit his son in the midriff. Richard staggered back, caught his heels on a rug and fell on his back. His face was screwed up with pain and he was gasping for breath.

Blood was pouring from his nose and mouth. Slowly he rolled over and began the laborious process of climbing upright.

'I guess . . . ' he wheezed, 'you've answered my question. Rich, powerful rancher pitted against defenceless farmers and smallholders. Brute force and ignorance — '

He got no further. Barrett Kerfoot lost it. He waded into his son, both hands pounding the youngster. Richard made no attempt to protect himself. He was driven remorselessly backwards, his father hitting out hard and viciously.

Martha Kerfoot was screaming as she watched her son being pounded. Richard was doing his best to remain upright as the bigger man attacked him. Under the barrage of punches he was driven against the wall. Barrett continued to work on him with his fists.

Martha could stand no more. She ran across to her husband and grabbed her his arm. She was screaming at him to desist. Barrett hardly paused in his efforts to beat his son to a pulp. He lashed out at his wife. His brawny forearm hit her on the side of the head and knocked her to the floor. Her screams were cut off abruptly.

Richard was unaware of his mother's efforts to save him. By now he was barely conscious. His face was a raw mess of bloody bruises and abrasions. He was held upright by the persistent hammering of the big fists.

Suddenly there were male voices yelling and hands pulling at the rancher.

'Pa, for God's sake, Pa, let up!'

'Pa, damnit all, Pa! Are you trying to kill the kid?'

His sons managed to pull the big man back from Richard, who slid down the wall to the floor. He lay there like one dead. Barrett senior blinked confusedly and stared at his sons as they pleaded with him.

'Damn milksop,' he muttered. He looked resentfully at the bloodied heap that was his son. 'There's always one of the litter that's no damn good.'

He allowed his sons to lead him across the room. Stewart was on one side and Ethan on the other. They held his arms and guided him to a chair. Stewart went across and knelt on the floor by his mother. With his help she sat up. Her eyes widened as she saw the huddled form of Richard.

'Oh my God, Richard,' she whispered.

Ethan came across and bent down over his injured brother. 'Jesus, what a mess!' He stood up. 'I'll get some help. Carry him up to his room.'

'No!' the explosive shout from Barrett Kerfoot brought all heads round to stare at the man who dominated their lives. 'I don't want that snivelling creature in my house. In fact I don't want ever to see him again. I disown him. He ain't no son of mine.'

'Jeez Pa, he's in a real bad way . . . '

'You hear me, boy! That's no son of mine. I want him outta here today.' Barrett stood and glared at his family. 'I'm going into town. When I return I want that cur off the Lazy K.'

'But Pa — '

'Am I master in my own house or not!'

The voice was thunderous. His family visibly shrank back. No one answered. Without another word the rancher strode from the room. His family listened in silence as doors slammed within the house till the rancher had gathered whatever he needed for his trip to town and left.

Martha was helped to a chair. Stewart fetched a glass of water. She could hardly hold the glass, she trembled so much. Stewart tried to help. Ethan tended to his battered brother. With Stewart's help they picked him up and laid him on a couch.

'Hell, what are we gonna do? He ain't in no fit state to go nowhere. He needs looking after.'

'We gotta do something. You know Pa. If he comes back and finds Richard still here he's liable to put a rope on him and drag him off the ranch.'

There was silence in the room.

Richard groaned and moved. His family stared helplessly at the bloodied wreck that was their brother.

'He was sweet on that dressmaker in town, Lavinia Wolfe.' The brothers turned to stare at their mother as she spoke. 'He went to funeral of that poor woman who was murdered by her husband,' Martha continued. 'Told me he went back to the house. Maybe she'll take him in.'

'I guess it's worth a try. We'll hitch up a wagon and drive him into town. If she's any sort of Christian woman she'll take him in.'

'Why was this Lavinia at the funeral of that sodbuster woman?' Stewart was looking down at the floor as he asked the question.

'They're related in some way. I don't really know. Right now I don't want to know.'

'Come on let's get this done and over with. Maybe Pa will have a change of heart and let Richard return sometime . . .'

18

'How much would you charge to store a saddle?'

The liveryman frowned at the man standing in the doorway. There was a saddle slung over one shoulder and a Winchester rifle dangling from a hand. The man had a dark beard with faint grey streaks and deep-set black eyes.

'What happened the horse?'

'Broke a leg.'

'Too bad. You wanna buy another?'

'Right now I ain't got no money to buy one. I'm needing a job. Know anyone as is hiring?'

The liveryman, a tall, weathered individual took off his hat and scratched his balding head. 'Julius Stiles has a small spread out to the west. He was in here earlier complaining he couldn't get no one to work with him regular. He don't pay much

144

but he'll more 'an likely take you on.'

'Julius Stiles. Where might I find him?'

The bearded stranger turned as he heard a sound behind him.

'Who's taking my name in vain?' The speaker was a man in his late forties with a pleasant open face and mild blue eyes. He strode inside and eyed up the stranger. 'What can I do for you, mister?'

'I was in need of a job.'

'You familiar with ranch work?'

'Sure.'

'You're hired. My wagon is outside. Tie your horse to it and you can ride in the wagon with me.'

'I ain't got no horse.'

Julius eyed up the stranger. His clothes were worn but clean. The man wasn't over big but somehow he exuded a sense of strength and stamina.

'We got horses aplenty back at the Circle A.'

The man with the saddle nodded and stepped outside. He did not go far but lingered by the door.

'You going to tell him, Julius, why you ain't got no hands out at the Circle A?'

'Goddamn your mouth, Seth.' There was a pause. 'I suppose you're right. I'd better tell him what he's letting himself in for.'

When the rancher came outside his new hand was sitting in the wagon. His saddle was on top of the stores Julius had bought. The wagon rocked slightly as Julius climbed up into the driver's seat. He gathered up the reins.

'What's your name fella?'

'Ray Daniels.'

'Ray, I gotta tell you what you're letting yourself in for.'

The man by his side stared ahead, waiting.

'I own the Circle A. It's only a small spread. Run five hundred head. Reason I ain't got no help is because of trouble with the Lazy K.' He looked sideways at his companion. 'You heard of the Lazy K?'

146

'Someone did mention it once but I know nothing about it.'

'It's the biggest ranch around here, run thousands of head. Got forty or fifty hands. Owned by a tough old coot name of Kerfoot. He got five sons and they're all as mean as the old man. Anyone as works for me or any other small rancher around here gets trouble from the Lazy K hands. Kerfoot aims to gobble up every spread within riding distance. On top of that he's harassing any sodbusters as try and settle. Once it's known you work for me they'll come at you like wolves after a wounded calf. They see you out riding they'll chase you. Come into town and they'll pick a fight. That's what you get with the Circle A: trouble and more trouble.' There was no response. Julius glanced sideways. 'Well, what you think?'

Those deep-set, unsettling eyes stared steadily back at him. 'Mister, I need a horse and I need a job. You offered me both. If you're prepared to take a chance

147

on me, I'll take a chance on you.'

As the wagon lumbered on its way Julius passed the time telling his passenger all about the ranch he was trying to keep out of the control of Barrett Kerfoot.

'You know, when I first came out here Barrett had the land but not many cattle. Then he began to accumulate a few extra head. I never could be sure but I reckon he was buying in stolen stock. I suppose he got a name for it and rustlers from all over would drive herds on to the Lazy K. I reckon they knew they had a sure-fire buyer in Barrett. You knew when a herd was delivered. His cowhands would be working round the clock, branding and the like. I have it on good authority from fellas as left his employ they were changing brands. Which is all well and good if you have a legit bill of sale for them cows you're branding. However nothing could be proved.'

'Kerfoot grew bigger and richer and the bigger he got the more grazing he needed. That's when the real trouble started. You ran a ranch nearby the Lazy K, things went wrong. Your cattle were stampeded. The Lazy K hands went out of their way to harass anyone as didn't work for them. Got so a fella couldn't go into town on Saturday night to let rip. He would end up with a sore head and it weren't from no liquor.'

'Well, your average hand ain't up for fighting and rowing all the time. He likes a drink and a wrestle with a bit of calico but he don't want his head busted open every time he rides into town. Cowhands began to drift. With no labour to work for them, most ranchers gave up. Barrett would buy up their property for a song.' Julius gave a long sigh at the end of this narration and lapsed into silence.

'How come you still here, Mr Stiles?'

'Call me Julius. I guess I'm just a stubborn cuss. Also I got a poorly wife. She got a lung disorder. Doctors told me she would improve if I came out here for the clear air. They were right too. She improved some. Still got some way to go but I have good hope for her. If you like your grub she's one helluva cook. She does stews and hotpots and roasts like they been delivered straight down from heaven.'

Anna Stiles was a delicate, auburn-haired woman with a shy smile. She met her husband on the porch and allowed him to peck her on the cheek before welcoming the new hand.

'If it's all right with you, Julius, I'll saddle up and take a ride around the ranch.'

'Sure. Take your pick of the bunch. They're all saddle broke.'

Very shortly after arriving on the Circle A the new hand was riding out to take up his duties. Julius continued to unload the supplies he had purchased in Consul. Suddenly he stopped as he had an uncomfortable thought. He turned to his wife.

'Durn me, I must be getting soft. I let that joker ride out on one of my horses.

What if that's all he wanted? What's to hinder him to keep on riding?'

'I was intrigued how he saddled up with only one hand,' his wife observed.

'One hand! Durn me, I never noticed that!'

She started to laugh then. 'Julius Stiles, you never were a judge of men.'

He grinned back at her. 'I'm a good judge of a woman, though.' By now he had moved close and embraced his wife.

'Julius, you work so hard and I'm not much help.'

'Hush, you're what keeps me going.' He stared off in the direction the new hand had taken. 'Ah well, maybe a one-handed man is better than no man at all.'

19

'There's riders coming, Lavinia.'

Lavinia nodded. She had already seen the body of horsemen.

'Probably from the Lazy K. I reckon they're on their way into town. I'll keep on at a steady pace. If they stop with us we'll just have to be civil to them.'

The riders drew close and when they realized only two women were in the buggy they formed a line and forced the vehicle to halt.

'This is a public highway,' Angelina stated politely. 'You're blocking our passage.'

Stewart Kerfoot edged forward. 'You're the hussies from the dress shop. I been in there a few times with my ma. That's a Lazy K buggy you're driving. Those horses have the Lazy K brand.'

'I know,' Angelina replied. 'Perhaps you forgot it was you and your brother delivered the buggy when you brought Richard to us.'

'Richard! He ain't a Kerfoot no more.' By now Stewart was alongside the buggy. Mounted he was on the same level as Lavinia. 'You the dummy? Well dummy down off that rig and I'll take it back to the Lazy K where it belongs.'

His companions sniggered.

'Like I say, this rig belongs to Richard. So if it pleases you and your cowhands to stand aside and allow us to go about our business.'

'Am I gonna pull you down off that rig or are you gonna see sense and get down your own selves'

As he spoke Stewart reached out towards Lavinia. There was a sudden movement from the girl and the cowboy found himself staring into the business end of a small revolver.

'What the — ?'

'Lavinia!' Angelina screamed. 'Don't shoot him!'

Stewart paused, frozen in the act of

153

reaching for the dressmaker.

'Mr Kerfoot, please don't make any sudden moves or it might be your last. Miss Lavinia was attacked by a couple of bad 'uns a while back. They beat her real bad. That's how she lost her speech. Ever since she has this fear that she might be attacked again. She already shot a fella back in Virginia.'

Stewart was staring with some apprehension at the gun aimed squarely at him. Angelina leaned across her companion and reached out a hand.

'Just hand me your reins, Mr Kerfoot. Do it real careful and slow. Now don't shoot, Lavinia. Mr Kerfoot don't mean no harm. He's only fooling. Hand me the reins now, like a good fella.'

Stewart could not take his eyes off the gun held rock steady in the hands of the young woman. Slowly he did as he was told, reaching his reins across. Angelina took the leathers and deftly tied them to the front bar on the buggy.

'Now, tell your friends to ride on into

town. Tell them to go real steady and not do anything to spook Miss Lavinia. She not right in the head since she took that beating. Lavinia, hang on in there. No shooting mind.'

'Damn you, I ain't doing no such thing!' Stewart snarled.

'Lavinia . . .'

Angelina made a grab for the gun. There was a sudden report. Kerfoot's hat was snatched from his head by an invisible hand. He jerked back, his eyes wide and frightened. His mount tried to shy away from the sudden noise of the gunshot. With the reins fastened to the buggy it did not get anywhere.

'Damnit Kerfoot, stay still!' Angelina yelled.

The man tried to restrain his frightened horse. He never took his eyes off the gun pointed steadily at him.

'The damn gunshot spooked my horse. I can't keep him quiet,' he yelled back, frightened out of his wits.

'I told you she ain't quite right in the head. I'm doing my best to keep you from being shot and her from being arrested for killing you.'

It was a convincing act on Angelina's part. The young rancher managed to quieten his horse and sat motionless, hypnotized by the black bore of the small gun pointed unerringly at him.

'Fellas, better do as she says and ride on into town. I'll join you as soon as I can.'

The cowboys did as they were told and filed past, glaring with sullen anger at the young women who had bested them. Angelina watched them all the way and leaned from the buggy to keep them under observation when they were past.

A good ten minutes ticked by before Angelina relaxed. All that time no one spoke a word. Lavinia's gun never wavered. Kerfoot sat quiet, licking his lips from time to time. At last Angelina reached across and released the man's reins.

'Now Mr Kerfoot, just you ride away real careful. I can't guarantee Miss

Lavinia will allow you to ride away without putting a hole in you somewhere. Don't look around and when you think you're far enough away dig those spurs in and ride like the devil is after you.'

The females watched him ride away. When he did as instructed and fled down the trail they collapsed back in the seat in sudden laughter.

'Damn me, Lavinia, Belle Starr has nothing on you when it comes to putting the frights up someone.'

Lavinia pulled her pad out. *What do you mean, telling them I weren't right in the head? I'm giving you your notice right now.*

Suddenly they were in each other's arms laughing hysterically.

'They'll be writing stories about you, Lavinia. The gun-slinging seamstress from Consul.'

Lurid stories of the Wild West, Lavinia wrote. *The Black Angel and gun-crazy Lavinia.*

It was some minutes before they were

composed enough to continue their journey. The objective of the trip was the Wolfe homestead where Lavinia's Aunt Gabrielle had met such a terrible end.

'What on earth's he doing?' Angelina asked shading her eyes against the light and peering ahead.

Richard Kerfoot looked up from his exertions, turned and waved. He walked down to the front of the house carrying a hoe as the women pulled up.

'Richard, what in God's name are you doing?' Angelina called.

'Miss Angelina, I can't just sit around any more. I was only working in the vegetables. I aim to get this place shipshape again.'

'You ain't right recovered yet,' Angelina scolded.

Richard was staring at Lavinia. 'Miss Lavinia, sure is good to see you again.'

'We brought you some food,' Angelina jumped down and rummaged in the buggy.

Richard moved up and held out his

hand to assist Lavinia to alight. Blushing furiously she reached out and took hold of his hand. When she was on firm ground the youngsters stared at each other for a few moment before Lavinia broke away and went round to assist Angelina. In spite of her preoccupation in unloading a basket of food Angelina noticed this little byplay. Lavinia's blushes had not quite faded when she came to Angelina's assistance.

'Are you hungry?'

'Could eat a roast ox and then look round for its mother.'

The basket of food was carried inside and the trio gathered round for a meal.

'We had a run-in with your brother Stewart today. He wanted to take the buggy from us. Claimed it was Lazy K property. Lavinia here held him off with her gun.'

Richard's jaw dropped. 'Oh no. That's terrible. You have risked so much for me already. Letting me live here and nursing me after my run-in with Pa.'

'We only did what any decent people would have done. Remember the good book, Richard. 'Do this to the least of my brethren and you do it to me.''

Lavinia was scribbling in her note pad. *Now that you're on the road to recovery, Richard what do you intend doing?*

'I'm glad you asked that, Lavinia. I know you told me you don't believe the terrible thing your uncle is supposed to have done. That being the case some day he will return. With your permission I would like to look after this place till he does turn up.'

Richard did not add that his real motive for the request was that it was his best chance of staying in touch with Lavinia. The girl's response was instantaneous.

Of course, you can stay as long as you want. We'll come out as often as we can to help.

And Richard, even though he had lost his family and his inheritance and was stuck on an isolated smallholding felt an immense surge of joy. The smile he turned on Lavinia reflected his elation. Lavinia looked away and was filled with an immense sense of sadness.

20

The new hand at the Circle A worked steadily for a goodly part of the morning. He was repairing fencing that bordered Lazy K range.

'You see riders coming at you jump on that bronco and head for home as fast as it'll take you,' Julius advised. 'Don't worry about the tools. Tools I can replace. Help is a damn sight harder to come by. Like I told you, those Lazy K riders are a mean bunch. They think it fun to break limbs and heads.'

Zacchaeus Wolfe, or Ray Daniels as he now thought of himself, heard the thunder of hoofs and glanced up at the riders coming fast towards him. Instead of taking his employer's advice and running for home he carried on knocking the fence post into the dirt.

There were three of them. Stewart

Kerfoot with two cowboys. All were armed with six-shooters. Zacchaeus had off-saddled his mount and the rifle was still in the scabbard. He made no move towards it. The riders pulled up a dozen yards or so from where he was working. Zacchaeus paused in his work and squinted up at the newcomers.

'Howdy,' he greeted them.

'We don't like fences, fella,' Stewart Kerfoot asserted. 'An' more important we don't like fellas as put them up.'

Zacchaeus shrugged. 'Never met a ranch hand yet as liked fences.'

The rider unslung his rope, shaking out the coils. With an expert flick of his arm the loop curled out and settled neatly over the post Zacchaeus was working on. With a quick haul on the reins the post was jerked out and dragged a few yards. Grinning widely Stewart pulled the post to him and leaned down to release his lariat. His mistake was in taking his eye off the man who was to be the next target for his rope.

Only a few yards separated the horseman and the fence-mender. The hammer flew across the short distance and smashed into Stewart's head as he leaned down to recover his rope from the fence post. He grunted and fell sideways. His horse, startled by the sudden movement of its rider, wrenched back and Stewart tumbled from his mount.

Stewart's companions were recovering from their surprise and grabbed at their sidearms. The guns were coming up and one of the men got off a shot. Zacchaeus stepped over to his saddle. With a quick movement he pulled the Winchester and had it pointing at the riders. The rifle crashed out twice in quick succession.

One man tumbled from the saddle with a bullet in the shoulder, the other yelled out as shell gouged a lump out of the hand holding his pistol. The weapon fell to the dirt and he bent over holding his injured paw and cussing loudly.

Stewart Kerfoot sat up and dazedly looked around him. The man by the fence stood immobile, the rifle casually pointed in the direction of the three injured cowboys.

'What the hell you mean pulling a gun on us?' Stewart yelled as soon as he saw his companions nursing their wounds and realizing what had happened. 'We ain't no range bums. I'm Stewart Kerfoot of the Lazy K.'

'Mister, I don't care who you are. I ain't the kind of man you mess with.' He walked slowly over to the trio who by now were glaring at him with sheer hatred. 'You unbuckle that gunbelt.'

'Like hell . . . ' Stewart began but got no further.

The rifle was suddenly in his face. A pair of flint-hard eyes stared out at the youngster. Quickly Stewart Kerfoot unbuckled.

'You other two leave those irons where they lie. Then fork them horses and be on your way.'

They glared sullenly at him, unwilling to comply. The fence-mender raised the rifle. That was a convincing reason for doing as they were told. The man with the bullet in his shoulder had trouble mounting.

'Help me, Stewart,' he whined.

Kerfoot went to his aid. When they were mounted they glared at their adversary.

'What about our six-shooters?'

Zacchaeus set his rifle down, picked up the weapons one by one and flung them far out in the direction he figured the horsemen would be riding.

'Pick them up on your way. Don't ever come back this way. You got off lightly this time.'

Sullenly they rode away, pausing only while Stewart climbed down and collected the weapons. He had difficulty in finding them in the long grass. All the while he searched he cursed steadily. At last they were on their way. Stewart Kerfoot turned in the saddle.

'Mister, you're dead. Nobody messes with Lazy K.'

'Seems I've heard about my demise

somewhere afore,' he muttered. 'I ain't seen the obituary notice so I ain't climbing in no grave just yet.'

He hauled the uprooted post back to the fence line. Stewart had been so shocked by the outcome of the encounter he had forgotten to recover his lariat. Zacchaeus coiled the rope, tossed it beside his saddle and began work again. He looked up as hoof beats once again disturbed the quiet of the day. Zacchaeus squinted in the direction of the sound and spotted his boss, Julius Stiles, riding hard in his direction.

'Damn me, I sure hope he brought some lunch.'

'Ray,' Julius called as soon as he was within range. 'Are you all right? I thought I heard gunfire.'

'Howdy, Julius. Sure I'm all right. I was just shooting at some snakes as come bothering me.'

'Snakes!' growled Julius. 'Snakes don't come about here with no reason.' Then he saw the dust in the distance and frowned. 'Is them riders coming or going?'

'I don't reckon they know themselves. One has a busted head.' Zacchaeus hefted the hammer he had downed the Lazy K rider with. 'One has a bullet in his shoulder and the other will have bother holding a gun for a while.'

Slowly Julius dismounted. 'Lazy K?' he queried.

'Afraid so.'

'Don't tell me you sent them off with their tail between their legs?'

'Afraid so.'

Suddenly Julius slapped his thigh and chortled. 'Damn my eyes, I'd a liked to a seen that! You sure one cool sonovabitch, Ray Daniels.' Suddenly he sobered. 'They'll not take kindly to being bested. They're liable to come back with reinforcements. Or else they'll lie in wait for you and ambush you, maybe in town or out here.'

Zacchaeus paused with the hammer poised above the fence post. Slowly he lowered his hand.

'Have I brought trouble on you, boss?'

Julius was shaking his head. 'Not on me but on yourself. They don't harass me, just my ranch hands. Barrett Kerfoot figgers if I have no help then I'll give up on the Circle A. They'll target you till they drive you off. If you wanna quit now and save yourself a lot of trouble I won't blame you.'

A pair of jet-black eyes stared back at the rancher.

'I ain't no quitter. If you want me to stay on there's one question I need to ask you.'

'Ask away.'

'Did you bring out my lunch?'

21

The two women had rummaged around the cabin and found a couple of aprons. Now they were busy washing and cleaning inside and outside the house that had belonged to Zacchaeus Wolfe and his wife Gabrielle. Richard had continued working with the hoe. In spite of his straitened circumstances he felt happier than he had for a long time.

The three young people paused in their labours as they heard the wagon approach. Lavinia felt for the reassuring touch of the small gun she carried in her pocket.

She had carried the weapon ever since being attacked by the brutal sons of Tamara when she had lived back in Virginia. She knew she would never submit again to such an attack.

The wagon pulled up and Lavinia relaxed as she recognized Adrian

Launder, the man who had assisted at the funeral of her Aunt Gabrielle. Beside the smallholder sat a younger version of Adrian. Lavinia guessed this was his son.

'Howdy, Miss Lavinia, Miss Angelina,' the man called before jumping down and smiling broadly at the women. 'I was just coming over to make sure everything was all right here. Ever since the killing we been nipping over once or twice a week to look after the place.'

By now Richard was walking down from the garden.

'Oh, by the way this is my son, Samuel.'

Wearing bib-and-brace overalls, the young man with lean features and curly brown hair jumped down. He stood with an awkward smile, not looking at the women. Adrian's smile faded when he recognifed the youngster coming down from the garden.

'Kerfoot, what's that spoiled young fool doing here?'

Richard was near enough to hear the muttered remark. 'Howdy, Mr Launder,' he said choosing to ignore the insult.

The man looked critically at Richard. 'What happened to your face, young man? Looks like a boar's been stomping all over it.'

Richard's face still showed the marks of the terrible beating his father had dished out to him. The youngster shrugged but did not enlighten the farmer. An awkward silence followed. Angelina came to the rescue.

'Won't you join us for coffee, Mr Launder? I reckon it's time we had ourselves a little break.'

They all trooped inside where Angelina served up coffee.

'Where's your son got to, Mr Launder?' Angelina asked, looking around the room.

'Samuel's a mite shy, especially around females. He don't have no conversation. That boy's always working. I told him time and time again he's gotta get out more and mix with young'uns his own age.'

'I'll take him out his drink.'

Angelina disappeared out the door with a mug.

'I ain't being impolite, son, but what's going on here? I ain't known a Kerfoot get his hands on a hoe afore.'

'You ain't got much of a regard for the Kerfoot family. Well, it might interest you to know my old man disowned me. Whether that still makes me a Kerfoot or not I ain't sure.'

'Disowned you! How come?'

'Last time we met, you told me to ask my father about destroyed crops and fired barns. Well, foolishly I asked him just that. Now I'm living here on the charity of Miss Lavinia. I ain't got nowhere else to go.'

Launder opened his mouth to say something, then closed it again. He glanced from Lavinia to Richard and back again. 'Dang me, if that don't beat all. Son, I'd like you to accept my apology. Seems as I gave you some wrong advice.'

'Mr Launder, I don't know. Right now I'm confused. I enjoy working out here, getting my hands dirty. The only thing is I don't know much about growing things. I only know horses and cattle. I used to look after the remuda for the Lazy K. It's all I ever wanted to do, work with horses. Now I got a buggy and team my brothers stole off the Lazy K for me and that's all. If my father finds out about that he might come out here and take even that away.'

'Son, I feel a mite responsible for your plight.' Launder was regarding the youngster thoughtfully. 'My boy out there knows all there is to know about farming. I reckon I can spare him a couple of days a week to come over and help out. When we heard what happened to Gabrielle and with Zacchaeus missing we took the animals to care for at our place. There's a herd of milk cows and some horses, so it ain't as if you got no livestock at all. There was goats but the danged things wouldn't allow us to catch them.'

'Mr Launder, that is mighty kind of you. I would appreciate some help.' Richard held out his hands. Lavinia gasped when she seen the raw state of them with busted blisters. 'As you can see I ain't used to digging or hoeing.'

The homesteader suddenly started laughing. 'Sorry, son,' he managed between guffaws. 'You got hands to match your face. And anyway, forget all this mister business. I'm just plain Adrian.' He got to his feet. 'Thanks for the coffee.' Still chortling he went to the door. He stepped outside, then stopped abruptly, effectively blocking the exit. 'Well, I'll be, would you look at that!'

Lavinia and Richard both came to the door at the same time. They had to peer over the farmer's shoulder to see what he was exclaiming about. Inadvertently their arms touched as they crowded into the doorway. Thinking the other was not aware of their intentions they leaned gradually towards each other. The heightened sense of warmth as they touched was dizzying for them both. It was moments before either could concentrate sufficiently to ask what was taking Launder's attention.

'It's Samuel. Just look at that young female talking to him.'

The couple behind Launder were forced to push further into the doorway in order to peer past him. This brought them even closer together. Unbeknownst to the other each was becoming quite light-headed with this enforced contact. They were looking out but were not taking much notice of what was going on.

Sitting in the cart was Samuel. Perched beside him chattering away was Angelina. Samuel was staring raptly into her face. Angelina's countenance was animated as she spoke and her hands were moving to illustrate her words.

'I just don't believe it. Wait till I tell his ma. She'll think I made it up.'

The young man and woman crowded into the doorway behind him glanced sideways at each other. Lavinia's eyes were aglow with some inner warmth. Richard had an almost uncontrollable desire to take Lavinia in his arms and press her even harder against him.

'Well, much as I hate to break up this happy little get-together, it's time we were heading back.'

Launder stepped into the yard and coughed discreetly. It was the signal for both couples to break apart. Side by side, Richard, Angelina and Lavinia stood in the yard and waved goodbye. They were still waving when the cart disappeared in the distance.

What were you telling him? Lavinia wrote in her notebook.

'Just talking about myself. When I come out with the coffee he seemed so shy and helpless I just started talking.' Angelina's eyes held a dreamy look. 'I can only remember some of what I was saying. It just seemed right to sit there and talk. He was such a good listener. He never once interrupted.'

Angelina missed the secret smile that passed between her companions.

22

'You use a sidearm?'

'Some.'

'I got a spare holster and gunbelt. If you care to have it you're welcome to it. Are you sure you wanna go into town?'

Zacchaeus shrugged. 'There's some things I need and I just don't like to hide out on the ranch. But if you want I'll stay here.'

'Anne has something for you. Come on in the house.'

Anna Stiles was smoothing out the material of a shirt she had laid out flat on the table. She smiled at the new man when he stepped inside, followed by her husband.

'Ma'am.'

'Ray, please don't take offence at what I made you.'

She held up the shirt, made of a fine black material with silver buttons. From one sleeve hung a glove stitched in place. The glove had been filled out so it looked like a hand dangling from the sleeve.

'I shaped the hand with bone. Keeps it rigid. Makes it more realistic. It's . . . it's to disguise your lack of a hand . . .'

She hesitated, watching his face. Slowly he walked forward, reached out and touched the glove, felt the rigidity of the filling. The cabin faded. He was standing by a forge. The blacksmith was strapping a metal artifice to his wrist.

'Ray . . . Ray, are you all right?'

Anna Stiles watched the light come back into his eyes.

'I'm sorry, Ray. It was tasteless of me to draw attention to your affliction.'

'No, ma'am, not at all. I'll be proud to wear this fine shirt. You shouldn't have gone to so much trouble.'

'My brother had an artificial leg. The kids called him such terrible names. I only thought this would help a little . . . Oh, I am a silly woman!'

He smiled at her. 'I'll wear this when I go into Consul.' He took the garment from her.

She smiled uncertainly back at him. 'Use the bedroom if you want. Try it on, see how it works.'

When he emerged from the bedroom, Anne and Julius watched anxiously as Zacchaeus held out his new hand.

'Feels good.'

'There is the mate to the glove if you want to wear that to balance the effect.'

Holding the spare glove in his teeth Zacchaeus deftly wriggled his hand inside it. With a mischievous grin he began to stroke his beard with the false hand.

'Can you tell the difference?'

Anna Stiles began to giggle. She had to sit down and pressed her hands against her mouth in an effort to stifle her mirth. Julius looked on with a bemused look.

'What's so funny?'

When she looked at her husband's face Anne went off again.

'Dang me, if I ever understood the female sense of humour. Come on, Ray, perhaps on the trip to town you can explain it to me.'

Maybe it was because it was Friday that Consul was brisk. Wagons and saddle horses were tethered all along the street. Julius drove to the livery. The liveryman was an old friend and they exchanged views on the weather, the price of feed and local gossip.

'Ray, I gotta go to the bank and then stock up on coffee and flour and a few essentials. With an extra mouth to feed, Anne's running out of stuff. Where will you be?'

'I was gonna buy a handgun but on account of you loaning me one I'll postpone that. I do need shells for my rifle. After that I guess I'll mosey down the saloon. I ain't had a drink in a coon's life.'

'Hell, I'll buy the shells. After all, it was defending my property you fired off them rounds. It seems only fitting I replace them.'

Zacchaeus nodded. 'I'll not argue with that. You're a fair man, Julius. I reckon you and me'll rub along just fine.'

'See you later. Oh, just one thing. Keep an eye out for them Lazy K hands. If any of them rannies spot you they're sure to wanna get their own back.'

Zacchaeus brandished his new hand in a dismissive gesture and set off towards the saloon. On the way he passed Lavinia's Fashions without a second glance. Perhaps, even had his niece caught sight of Zacchaeus, in all likelihood she might not have recognized the black-garbed, bearded man ambling past the dress shop.

Above the saloon was a mural by the same artist who had painted the Parisian scene for Lavinia's Fashions. An elephant was dunking its trunk into a beer barrel while a monkey was sitting on its back with a glass of spirits in its paw.

The Elephant and Monkey was

moderately busy, for the day was getting late. As the sunlight hours diminished more and more ranch hands would drift in for the Friday-night shindig.

A poker school was in progress with several players engrossed in the cards. Other customers stood or sat nursing drinks. Some glanced idly at the newcomer. Zacchaeus chose a place along the bar that fronted on to a large mirror. From this vantage point he could view the barroom without having to turn round.

'Whiskey, and leave an extra glass. I'm expecting a friend.'

After downing the first glass he prepared a quirly. Even one-handed he was adept at rolling his own. The barman supplied a lucifer and Zacchaeus stood relaxed, contentedly smoking and taking his time with his second drink. There was a sudden stir of movement by the card table.

'That's him! That's the varmint as threw down on us.'

The card-players were breaking up from the table and turning towards Zacchaeus. He did not move from his position but used the mirror to study the men who were taking the sudden interest in him. One had a bandaged head and another a bandaged hand while a third had his arm in a sling. Zacchaeus sighed deeply.

'So much for a quiet drink,' he muttered.

The men were standing up now. Slowly the group moved across the saloon to stand behind Zacchaeus.

'Someone fetch the sheriff. That's the booger as ambushed us.'

One of the cowhands detached from the group and vanished out through the door. Zacchaeus slowly turned to face the row of Lazy K men. His cigarette was wedged between the fingers of his false hand. He raised the hand to his mouth and sucked in a lungful of smoke.

'Mister, we're holding you till the sheriff gets here. You gonna come quietly or do we have to pistol-whip you?' It was the cowboy with the bandaged head that spoke.

'Stewart Kerfoot, I remember you. Broke my fence. When I objected you run away so fast you left your lariat behind. You can come and fetch it any time you like.'

Someone in the body of the saloon tittered. Kerfoot was getting red in the face.

'How's your head, Stewart? Accidents will happen when you interfere with a man at work.'

'Damn you, you'll be laughing on the other side of your face when the sheriff arrests you for unlawful wounding.'

As if on cue the saloon door opened and Sheriff Saul Harrell walked inside.

'What's all this, Stewart? Ben tells me you got the fella as ambushed you the other day.' Sheriff Harrell planted himself in front of Zacchaeus. 'Mister, I'm arresting you for attempted murder.'

Neither the sheriff, nor indeed any of the assembled men, associated this bearded stranger with the man they had transported across the prairie. When the posse dumped Zacchaeus Wolfe he was all but dead. As far as the sheriff was concerned, by now the sodbuster's bones would be bleaching in the woods. There was no reason in the world to suggest the lawman and this saddle bum had ever met before.

Cold black eyes stared out at the lawman. Zacchaeus was recalling what Rose had said, about how he came to be dumped for dead out in the hills.

'There was a lawman with them there critters. He was telling them what to do.'

23

Sheriff Harrell did not anticipate any bother with his victim. The man he was confronting was of slight build and did not appear in any way dangerous. On the rare occasion when he had to tackle drunks and troublemakers his size and badge were usually enough to cow them.

The sheriff had an easy living in Consul. In a town where Barrett Kerfoot was the real law the sheriff had only one tenet. All that was needed was to follow orders. One of those orders was to take for granted the word of anyone connected with the Lazy K. When called upon to arrest the man Stewart Kerfoot claimed had ambushed him he came readily enough.

'You hear me, fella?'

'Sheriff, if I had attempted to murder these fellas they would be out there

187

now, feeding the buzzards.'

Sheriff Harrell blinked. This wasn't how it should be. 'I'm afraid you'll have to let the judge decide that. In the meantime hand over that sidearm and come quietly.'

The bearded stranger frowned. 'That being the case you'll havta arrest these fellas as is accusing me. Fair is fair. The judge will have to decide if they are telling the truth also.'

The sheriff smiled. 'You don't understand. These are Lazy K cowboys. It's your word against theirs. Like I say, come quietly, otherwise I might havta get rough.'

'There is no law but the law of Lazy K?'

'What?'

'Hell, Sheriff, stop this fooling around and arrest the sonovabitch.' Stewart called. 'We'll back your play.'

There was a sudden movement and the men behind the sheriff were pulling guns. Before Sheriff Harrell could react the bearded man stepped in close and something hard jabbed into the lawman's midriff.

'Sheriff, you tell those cowboys to put up those irons or you're looking at a severe case of lead poisoning.' Zacchaeus's eyes were only level with the sheriff's chin. Sheriff Harrell stared down into twin black pits and was suddenly afraid.

'This ain't the way to do it, fella.' There was a distinct tremor in the lawman's voice. 'There's no need for no shooting.'

'You tell that to them fellas with their guns out.' The voice was cold and emotionless. 'They start shooting you're the first casualty.'

'Boys, do as the gent says and put those irons away.'

'Hell, Sheriff, you gonna let him get away with this?'

'Damnit, Stewart, do as he says!'

There was a note of panic in the sheriff's voice. The pressure of the gun in his guts was very insistent. For a moment the tension could be felt as the cowboys weighed up the options.

'He won't shoot no lawman!'

'Try me. You fellas should know I shoot straight enough. I can't miss lard-guts at this distance; the gun's pressing against his innards. The bullet might just plough on through, come out the other side and hit some of you. Then when fat guts here falls to the ground I'll just carry on shooting. Counting the sheriff I should get at least another four afore you gun me down.'

None of them was brave enough to put this boast to the test. When it was only the sheriff in the firing line they had been tempted to shoot it out with the bearded stranger. Now that he was telling them calmly he would gun down as many of them as he could before they got him they were fearful. Men who are used to hunting in packs are cowards at heart. They wavered and were lost.

'Please fellas,' Sheriff Harrell croaked. 'I ain't aiming to take no gut shot. Do as he says and back away.'

One by one they sheathed their irons and shuffled back.

'Sheriff, I just come in here to enjoy a quiet drink. I would be obliged if you would join me.'

'Sure ... sure thing, fella, just ... just put that gun away. I don't mind having a drink with you.'

Zacchaeus backed to the bar. 'Stay close, Sheriff. I want you to act like I'm your long-lost brother, we'll be that close.'

The sheriff bellied up to the bar. Zacchaeus moved with him and, shielded by the bulk of the lawman, put his gun back in its holster.

'Pour a drink for yourself, Sheriff, and one for me. I like to keep a hand free in case I havta shoot a few coyotes.'

Sheriff Harrell poured. His hand was shaking so much some of the whiskey spilled on the bar.

'Seeing as you're sheriff, I suppose I oughta report an odd thing I came across in the hills back of here.'

The sheriff downed his drink and stared at the man beside him. Zacchaeus had turned his back on the room. His eyes were alert as he watched the reflection in the glass of the sullen Lazy K bunch.

'There was the remains of a cowpoke and his horse. The fella hadda bad head wound. The horse had broke a leg. I suppose as the law around here you oughta go on out there and investigate, in case there was foul play involved.'

Zacchaeus could feel the tension building in the man beside him. The sheriff had gone a shade pale.

'Have another drink, Sheriff. You look as if you'd seen a ghost.'

The bottle clinked against the tumbler as the lawman poured. More whiskey spilled.

'Sheriff, take it easy. You're tipping out more of that there rotgut than you're drinking. Maybe you oughta drink from the bottle. That way you mightn't spill.'

While Zacchaeus was talking he was keeping an eye on the Lazy K riders.

They were whispering and glowering across at him. Two of them broke away. Zacchaeus tensed but the men went out the back way. He guessed they were either going to fetch help or were planning on setting up an ambush for when he left the saloon.

Sheriff Harrell was staring at Zacchaeus with slack mouth and uneasy expression. He had not responded to the tale of the body in the hills.

Zacchaeus decided it was time to cut and run before the Lazy K men rallied or brought up reinforcements. A small victory had been won. He was almost certain from the sheriff's reactions that he was the lawman Rose had seen directing the disposal of the wounded man and his horse. He had much to think about.

'Perhaps I should take care of that pistol you're wearing,' Zacchaeus suggested. Without waiting for a reply he reached out and removed the sheriff's pistol. If there was to be an ambush he did not want the sheriff loose with a loaded gun. 'I'll drop it into the office on my way outa town.'

Keeping a wary eye on the Lazy K crowd Zacchaeus backed slowly to the door. No one moved and no one made any attempt to stop him. He pushed out through the doors and cannoned into Julius.

'Ray, I was just coming . . . '

The rancher got no further. His words were cut off as shots rang out from the far side of the street. Julius grunted as the bullets hit him in the back. Zacchaeus grabbed at his boss and dropped to the boardwalk with the rancher. Even as he was easing the wounded man to a resting position he emptied the sheriff's gun in the direction of the alleyway from where he judged the shots had come. Tossing aside the empty gun he was up and sprinting across the roadway, oblivious of the shots coming his way.

He saw the outline of the ambushers and pulled his own pistol, the one given to him by Julius. He fired at the killers.

One of the men staggered out into the street clasping his hands to his body. He did not get far before he collapsed. The second man turned to run.

Zacchaeus hauled to a stop. He took his time and sighted on the fleeing gunman. Twice he fired and hit each time. The ambusher threw up his hands and pitched forward on to his face. Zacchaeus whirled to face the saloon. Julius Stiles, the man who had taken a chance on employing him, lay where he had fallen. The rancher was ominously still.

Zacchaeus knelt down beside the rancher. With some foreboding he felt for a pulse.

'Damn murdering dry-gulchers.'

The door to the saloon opened. Sheriff Harrell stood just inside the door, pointing a pistol at the kneeling man. The lawman had a triumphant look on his face.

'Drop that gun, you murdering booger. This time there is no doubting your guilt. You're caught red-handed.'

24

Zacchaeus slowly stood up. 'I don't suppose it would do any good to tell you the two bushwhackers as shot Stiles are lying in that alleyway across the road.'

'No one will believe that, you murdering sonovabitch', Sheriff Harrell sneered. 'Turn around, mister. Stewart, put these handcuffs on.'

Zacchaeus turned around as he was ordered. There was nothing else he could do. His own weapon was empty. The sheriff stood out of reach with his pistol trained on him. Stewart Kerfoot stepped out from behind the sheriff and with an exultant look on his face cuffed the hands together.

With Zacchaeus safely manacled Stewart stepped back a pace. Raising his boot he thudded it into the prisoner's back. Zacchaeus was catapulted out into the road. Unable to save himself he crashed face down on the dirt. Behind him men were spilling from the saloon. There was rough laughter and abuse from the sidewalk as Zacchaeus climbed awkwardly to his feet. It was no easy task with his wrists bound behind him. It was a source of great amusement for the crowd of onlookers.

It was a painful trip to the jail for Zacchaeus. Stewart Kerfoot and the surviving cowboys took great pleasure in kicking and tripping the manacled prisoner as they progressed down the street. When at last they got him to the cell he was filthy and bruised from the rough treatment.

'Now we got that ring-tailed gopher caged I guess its time for us to celebrate,' Stewart Kerfoot crowed. 'Sheriff, you joining us?'

'Sure thing, Stewart. I guess we all deserve a drink after this.'

Before leaving Stewart Kerfoot peered through the bars at the prisoner.

'You're gonna hang, cowboy. You're

gonna hang for the murder of Julius Stiles and my two buddies, Jacob Birch and Steve Hewitt.'

There was no response. Zacchaeus did not look up. He was slumped on the bunk the picture of despair, pathetic and bedraggled.

'Nobody, but nobody, messes with Lazy K, especially no saddle bum.'

'Stewart, you buying them drinks or are you going to hang around here all night?'

They went from the jail leaving the prisoner to contemplate his fate. For long moments he waited till he was certain they were gone. Then he set to work.

★ ★ ★

The Lazy K celebrations were going well. Stewart Kerfoot was generous with his old man's wealth. He ran up considerable tabs with the barkeeps happy to oblige. Barrett Kerfoot never quibbled over settling bills run up by his children.

'Who's coming with me to Marge Gordon's cathouse,' Stewart suddenly asked. 'Then we can come back to here and celebrate some more.'

'Sure thing, boss.'

Jason Lee and Merrit Chase got to their feet. They left behind Joe McDonald and George Rankin who were heavily into a poker game and did not fancy a trip to the whorehouse. Sheriff Saul Harrell was content to stay in the Elephant and Monkey. The events of the day had been unsettling. He needed alcohol to steady his nerves and then some.

When that cowpoke told him about discovering a body in the hills he had felt a shiver of fear. Then when the *hombre* had shoved a gun in his guts he had almost lost control of his bowels. The more he drank the more the fright receded. So he stayed on at the saloon and downed more whiskey to dull the edge of his fears.

Stewart and his lackeys stepped out from the saloon. They were about to start walking towards the bordello when Stewart paused. He held his hand up and hissed at his companions to be quiet. A buggy was passing in the street. Stewart drew back into the shadows of the walkway pulling Chase and Lee with him.

'It's them goddamn females from the dress shop,' he whispered. 'The ones as buffaloed us the other day. I got me an idea. Let's just follow those two jezebels.'

Buoyed up by his victory over the Circle A cowhand and fortified with whiskey, Stewart was in a reckless mood. He had a score to settle with those females. What better time than now to call them to account? Trying not to be too obvious the three drunken cowboys stalked the buggy.

The women, unaware that they were the targets of hidden eyes, blithely carried on. They had spent the day at the Wolfe homestead. The bonus for Angelina was that Samuel Launder was present. Four young people had spent the day together, working and getting to know each other and gradually loosing their awkwardness and shyness.

The buggy stopped at the livery. Seth the liveryman always cared for the horses and stabled them. He had waited for them to check in. As a rule they were never this late. He grumbled at them good-naturedly. They walked the short distance to the shop in silence. Lavinia could not speak and her notepad was useless in the dark.

It was as they were unlocking the door the shadows came out of the night and bundled them inside. Rough hands were clamped across the girls' lips to prevent them crying out. They were dragged through the shop and out into the rear. This was where the gowns were cut out and sewn together.

For Lavinia the suddenness and brutality of the attack was the reliving of a nightmare.

'Light the lamp there,' Stewart ordered. 'Let these fillies see what fine men they have netted.'

The oil lamp flared into life, showing the interior of the workshop. Stewart was holding Lavinia, pinioning her arms to her sides. Joe McDonald held Angelina with one arm while his spare hand was clamped across the girl's mouth. Both girls struggled wildly. Stewart let go of Lavinia long enough to punch her in the mouth. She gasped and staggered back. Kerfoot grabbed her again and prevented her falling.

'Give me a hand, here,' Jason Lee hissed as he struggled with Angelina.

Merrit Chase finished with the lamp and came to his companion's aid. He wrapped his arms around Angelina while Jason kept his hand in position across her mouth.

Angelina tried to kick Chase. He just grinned and smashed his head against her face. Angelina sagged in Jason Lee's arms. Blood poured from a cut on her forehead. Her eyes were wild and staring but still she did not give in. She drove an elbow into the man holding her mouth to prevent her crying out.

Chase grunted and started cursing. Merrit drew back slightly and drove a bunched fist into Angelina's midriff. She tried to double over with Jason Lee letting her go partway.

Stewart Kerfoot had pushed Lavinia against the wide bench the girls used for laying out the patterns for the dressmaking. He pressed his lips brutally against hers. She struggled but was helpless in his cruel grip.

Jason Lee and Merrit Chase were similarly molesting Angelina. The only sound in the back room of Lavinia's Fashions was the fevered grunts of the three men as they struggled to subdue the two women.

Outside in the night the town of Consul was at play. Saloons and brothels were doing a lively trade. It was Friday night and it seemed everyone was out to enjoy themselves. In the back room of Lavinia's Fashions two young women fought a forlorn battle against the brutal intentions of the men of the Lazy K.

25

Zacchaeus stood up from his seat on the bunk. For a moment he stayed still listening. The jailhouse seemed empty.

'Hi, anyone there?'

For a moment more he stood still, his head craned to one side as he listened. Satisfied no one was about he turned back to the bunk. His wrists were still manacled behind his back. He had to figure out a way to get rid of them. First he jerked his wrists hard apart trying to prise the false hand from its moorings. Anna Stiles's sewing was thorough. Tug and heave as he might, nothing shifted.

'Hell, I can't even take the damn shirt off.'

At last he lay on the bunk and began to slip his arms down underneath his rear end. It was slow and joint-wrenching but at last he pulled his arms to the front.

Kneeling down beside the bunk he grasped the base and lifted the wooden leg off the floor. Jamming his knee beneath the bunk to keep it off the floor he slipped his arms beneath the leg and lowered the whole thing again. The wooden leg of the bunk now held the manacles trapped.

He lay back and placed his boots against the edge of the bunk and began to heave. His face twisted up with the effort. As he pulled the pressure on his good wrist was extremely painful. Only the glove he wore saved him from even more damaging pain. Harder and harder he pulled. Nothing gave.

'Mrs Stiles, I sure wish you weren't such a good seamstress,' he gritted out.

The muscles on his shoulders and arms bulged against the material of the shirt. Sweat stood in beads on his forehead.

'Give damn you, give!'

There was a ripping sound and the material of the shirt split from the glove. Everything gave way and the carefully fashioned false hand fell to the floor. Zacchaeus lay for a moment, gasping from the intense exertions of the last few moments. The loose handcuff dangled from his good hand.

He picked up the ruined hand and paused as he saw the rods that had held the glove to the shirt. Thoughtfully he extracted a couple of knitting needles. One of these he slid up the sleeve of the torn shirt. The other he secreted in his clothes. Then he kicked the ruined hand beneath the bunk. Just then he heard the front door of the jail open.

Sheriff Harrell tottered inside the jailhouse. He had drunk so much at the Elephant he had begun to feel queasy.

'Damnit, I need something to sober me up,'

Back at the jail he kept a bottle of liquorice water that had proved its worth in the past. A few mouthfuls of that mixture were guaranteed to quell a man's rebellious stomach. Sheriff Harrell was rummaging about in the dark trying to find his medicine when he heard the voice calling.

'Hi there, is someone there?'

The sheriff paused in his efforts. 'Shut your damn mouth,' he yelled back.

'Goddamn it, I need the john. Damn your hide, I'm desperate.'

'So am I,' the lawman muttered. 'Where is that damned bottle?'

Back in his cell Zacchaeus was banging the manacles against the iron bars and pleading for help. Eventually his efforts were rewarded and the sheriff appeared, Colt in hand.

'Shut that damn caterwauling! My damn head aches. Stand back from the door.'

Zacchaeus backed to the rear of the cell. His arms were held behind him. There was nothing to suggest to his jailer he was not securely manacled. It took a couple of tries for the sheriff to get the key in the lock.

'Only you're gonna hang, I've a good mind to shoot you now for all the trouble you caused.'

'Sheriff, I just wanna go. Then you can shoot me.'

The cell door swung open. Sheriff Harrell backed up, his gun aimed at the prisoner. As Zacchaeus stepped out of the cell he brought his arm from behind his back and swiped at the sheriff's gun with the loose handcuff. Sheriff Harrell instinctively jerked back and pulled the trigger. Zacchaeus gasped aloud as the bullet ploughed a red-hot track along his ribs. He leaped forward and grappled with the lawman. The sheriff was against the wall. His attacker had grabbed the gun and was punching into the sheriff's gut with his bony stump. Sheriff Harrell was trying to bring the gun up to have another shot.

Zacchaeus was desperate. He was certain the shot would bring someone to investigate. He had to bring the struggle to a quick end. Suddenly he let go of the sheriff's gun, pulled out the knitting needle and plunged it deep into the sheriff's eye.

'Aaagh!'

The wounded man sagged and began to slide down the wall, moaning pitifully. His grip slackened on the gun and Zacchaeus snatched it from the lawman's hand. He smashed the weapon against the side of the lawman's head and the moaning stopped. Sheriff Harrell slid to the floor and ended up resting against the wall. Only a couple of inches of knitting needle were visible. The rest was buried inside the sheriff's head.

Quickly Zacchaeus ran to the front of the building. He stood against the wall by the door and waited. After a few moments, when nothing happened, he came to the conclusion the gunshot had gone unnoticed. No one was coming to investigate.

Cautiously he opened the front door and peered out. There were a few people in the street, obviously wondering where the shot had come from but no one came his way. He shut the door again and made his way back to the cell. Sheriff Harrell was still sitting slumped against the wall.

Zacchaeus stuffed the Colt in his waistband and grabbed up the bunch of keys. The handcuffs still dangled from his wrist but he did not waste time trying to remove them. His side was painful and he could feel wetness from the wound but he decided to ignore that for the moment. He slipped the bolts to the rear door and stepped out into the night.

Cautiously Zacchaeus walked along the back alleyway. His thoughts were to make his way to the livery stable and use his dead boss's wagon to get out of town.

'Damnit, I suppose no one has bothered to ride out to the Circle A and tell Mrs Stiles about her husband,' he muttered. It was a task he was not relishing. 'She'll more than likely blame me.'

A light was spilling out into the back alley from a building ahead. Zacchaeus slowed down and crept forward. He had to cross that band of light. It was a place of danger that might expose him to discovery. He heard a woman scream and a man's hoarse voice swearing. In spite of his own situation Zacchaeus had to look inside that building.

He flattened against the wall and inched forward till he could peer through the lighted window. The woman cried out again and there came the sound of a fist thudding into flesh.

Zacchaeus knew he should keep moving. He should ignore whatever was going on inside the house. There were enough troubles of his own to contend with. Any moment now someone might discover the injured sheriff and the hue and cry would go up.

Zacchaeus had not lingered to discover if Sheriff Harrell was alive or dead. As it was he did not care much either way. The sheriff and his cronies from the Lazy K had already condemned him. They had deliberately framed him for the killing of Julius Stiles. If they'd had their way he would have hanged for a murder he did not commit.

There was also the fact the sheriff was involved in some way in his own predicament. Sheriff Harrell had left him for dead out in the hills for reasons of his own. Zacchaeus wanted to know about that incident but he knew he had to leave it till a more convenient time.

Also he was wounded. The pain in his side was bearable but he could feel the wetness of the blood leaking from the wound. He did not think it was too serious. The bullet had scored along his ribs. However it did not do to leave a wound untended. The sooner he got help the better. There was the sound of scuffling inside the lighted room. Zacchaeus edged his head forward and peered through the window.

26

As soon as he viewed the scene inside the room Zacchaeus knew he was not going to walk away from this. The women he did not recognize, it was the men who grabbed his attention.

'Stewart Kerfoot and his unsavoury buddies,' he whispered.

The rancher was wrestling with a young white woman. Jason Lee and Merrit Chase were similarly engaged in grappling with a young black woman. The intentions of the men were plain, for they were yanking at the garments of the two females.

Kerfoot had managed to tear away a portion of the girl's dress. His companions were busily engaged tying a gag in place on the young black woman. Neither of the girls was making it easy for their attackers. The men were cursing roundly while punching the women. They were delivering fierce body blows and this punishment was taking its toll. It was obvious the girls could not take much more of this brutal treatment.

Zacchaeus had seen enough. He looked for and found a door. Carefully he tested the latch. He was in luck. The door opened under his touch. Zacchaeus pulled his gun, pushed open the door and stepped inside.

The white girl saw him first. Her eyes widened. Kerfoot noticed the change in her expression and whirled round. His mouth dropped open.

'Where the hell did you come from?'

'You got it in one. Hell!'

Drunk as he was, Kerfoot was quick. With a surprisingly swift movement he whirled about and reversed positions with the girl. Now he was behind her with her body shielding him from the intruder. His companions were mesmerized by the appearance of the man they thought was safely locked in jail. Kerfoot had his Colt out and pushed into the girl's chin. He was grinning in triumph.

'Drop the iron, cowboy, else I blow a hole in the whore's head.'

The girl was staring at Zacchaeus. He watched fascinated as she nodded to him. Shoot, the look seemed to be saying, don't mind about me.

Out of the corner of his eye Zacchaeus saw the cowboys with the black girl let her loose as their hands dived for their holstered weapons. He had no time to think. The target was small. Only a small portion of Kerfoot's face was visible. Zacchaeus fired.

The bullet smashed into Stewart Kerfoot's chin. It tore away his lower jaw and emerged behind his ear. The rancher jerked back and at the same time the girl threw herself forward. Stewart opened his mouth to scream but could only manage a muffled gurgle from his damaged jaw.

Zacchaeus fired again. His second bullet entered the wounded man's throat, went on through the soft tissue and came out at the back of his neck. Stewart staggered back and dropped from sight.

Chase and Lee had their pistols out and began firing. Bullets were buzzing around Zacchaeus but miraculously he was not hit. Mostly this was because the cowboys were drunk; they were also terrified after seeing their boss shot down. More important, the black woman they had been molesting grabbed up a steel rule used for marking out material and drove the end into Jason Lee's mouth. The sharp steel end split his lip and ploughed up into his gums. He wrenched away from her with a strangled yell. The bullets from his Colt went wild.

Even though he was under fire Zacchaeus coolly turned towards the two cowboys. Seeing Lee temporarily out of the action he fired at Merrit Chase, hitting him in the chest and driving him back into a stack of rolled cloth. Without pausing he put another two bullets into the injured Lee. And suddenly it was all over.

Jason Lee and Merrit Chase lay dead on the floor. Their boss, Stewart Kerfoot, was lying wounded with half his face missing. He had dropped his pistol and was sitting on the floor with his back against the wall. His eyes stared at Zacchaeus, wide and frightened. Zacchaeus did not know it then but his second bullet had clipped the rancher's spine. Stewart Kerfoot was partially paralysed. He would never again molest helpless women.

Before Zacchaeus could holster his weapon the white girl rushed across the room and threw her arms around him. Her companion had to step over the bodies of the dead cowboys to get to him.

'Zacchaeus, thank God you arrived when you did!'

Zacchaeus was staring in wonder at the girl as she spoke. She too was trying to embrace him.

'Where on earth have you been? We were worried sick about you. We thought you might be dead.'

'You know me?' he asked wonderingly.

'Why shouldn't I know you? That beard don't fool no one.'

Lavinia had by now released him. He gazed at the young woman. Her eyes were shining as she returned his gaze.

'You know me, too?'

She nodded and managed a smile.

Suddenly there were shouts from the street out front. Zacchaeus had no time to wonder about this new development. Swiftly he stepped across and doused the lantern.

'Keep quiet. If they find us here with those bodies we'll all be in trouble.' They could hear men calling to each other. 'Go through to the front and find out what's happening. Don't let anyone see you.'

Angelina did as he told her and went through to the shop. Lavinia had taken hold of his hand.

'You remember me?' he whispered.

She made no reply and he did not press the point. They stood close in the darkness and the feel of her hand in his comforted him.

Angelina came back in a short while. The shouting had faded.

'I guess they've all gone back to the saloons. The street seems clear. Oh, Zacchaeus it's so good to see you again.'

'There's things I gotta talk to you about. Before that we havta get rid of these bodies.' Zacchaeus pointed to Stewart. The man's head was tipped forward. A bubbling sound was coming from his ruined throat as his breath came and went. 'That fella is a Kerfoot. They seem to own the law about here. If they connect you to the killing we'll all hang for it.'

'What are we gonna do?'

'I think I know. You'll havta help.'

Lavinia held up Zacchaeus's hand. The cuff was still attached. Her eyebrows rose as she looked at him. Zacchaeus dug his hand in his pocket and produced the bunch of keys he had taken from the sheriff.

219

'Here, unlock that for me.' While she was finding the right key he explained what they had to do. 'I can't do it by myself.' He indicated the dark patch on his shirt. 'I've been wounded tonight. I think it's only a graze but it means I can't do this all on my own.'

One by one they carried the bodies out and ferried them along to the rear of the jailhouse. Zacchaeus found Sheriff Harrell where he had left him. The lawman was snoring loudly. When the girls saw the knitting needle protruding from his eye they gasped in shock.

'What happened to him?' Angelina whispered.

'I think someone musta needled him,' Zacchaeus replied.

Lavinia gave him a reproving look.

They laid Stewart Kerfoot on the bunk inside the cell. Blood from his wounds had soaked his shirt. He was still alive but unconscious. Zacchaeus tore up some of the bedding and tied it in place around the ruined jaw and neck. He wasn't sure why he did it but some sense of humanity prompted him to help his enemy.

It's more than the sheriff did for me when he dumped me in the hills to die, he thought.

When they dragged the still snoring lawman inside the cell he curled up on the floor and carried on snoring. Zacchaeus debated whether to remove the knitting needle and then decided if the sheriff survived it might be better if someone medically qualified did it. The dead cowboys they dumped inside the back door of the jail.

By the time all this was completed Zacchaeus was staggering with exhaustion. His wound was throbbing and his shirt was soaked in blood. Seeing his plight the girls took an arm each and supported him back to the shop.

'I gotta lie down somewhere,' he said.

'Not before I attend to that wound,' Angelina insisted. 'We'll help you upstairs. Lavinia, get the kettle boiled. We'll need hot water.'

27

'So I was dumped in the hills for dead. I surely believe if Rose Perry hadn't found me I would have died out there. Rose claimed she had seen a lawman with the men who dragged me out there. I'm pretty sure that was Sheriff Harrell. Prior to that I can remember nothing.'

Zacchaeus was sitting on a chair while the two girls worked on him. They had cleansed the wound and anointed it with salve. Now they were busy winding a long measure of flannel cloth around his chest to keep the cotton dressing in place.

Angelina and Lavinia looked at each other as if silently conferring.

'Nothing?' Angelina asked without looking at Zacchaeus.

'Nothing. Now tell me, who am I supposed to be.'

'Your name is Zacchaeus Wolfe. You are a homesteader. A week or so ago your wife, Gabrielle was found murdered. She had been battered to death. You were accused of her murder. Barrett Kerfoot put up a reward for your capture. It looks as if the sheriff felt safe posting the reward if he believed you were dead.'

'I had a wife! None of this I remember.'

Lavinia was scribbling in her pad. *We'll take you out to the homestead. Maybe it'll help you remember.*

'I don't think you should be associating with me. Once Kerfoot is discovered in the jail along with the sheriff all hell will be raised. Barrett Kerfoot will double that reward on my head. He'll pull his crew off cow-herding and send them after me. While it's dark I'll make my way outta town. I'll take the wagon that Julius Stiles left in the livery. I havta go out to the Circle A and tell his wife . . . widow.'

You're going nowhere, Uncle Zac.

223

Now that we've found you again I'm not letting you out of my sight.

'You don't understand. I can't just ride about where I want. Come daylight they'll be combing the country for my hide. If I'm found with you they'll rope you in as well. Just look at what them fellas were doing to you. They're all the same at the Lazy K. They're above the law. They'll hang me and they'll hang you alongside me.'

Zacchaeus made efforts to arise from the couch. A pair of hands gently pushed him back.

When you're ready we'll take you out to your home. We have a buggy. You'll be hiding in the back. It's the only way. If we get you back in your home it might just trigger off memories.

While she was writing in her little pad Zacchaeus had a chance to study her. If this was his niece he was fortunate indeed to have such a beautiful young woman for family.

When they set out in the morning there was such a buzz of activity in the town that the dressmakers drove out of town in Richard Kerfoot's buggy without anyone taking much notice of them. Once away from the town Zacchaeus sat up from his uncomfortable and stifling hiding place. The girls had draped a rug over him.

None of them had slept much after the disturbing events of the evening. Most of the journey was taken in silence each lost in their separate thoughts.

Richard Kerfoot was working when the buggy rolled up to the cabin. He had driven the milk herd down to the corral by the house and was busy milking. When he saw the buggy pull up he waved cheerily to them.

'I'll be with you presently. Just finish Sapphire for now.'

Since the Launders had returned the animals they had rescued, Richard was getting to grips with the daily task of milking them. To the girls' amusement he had named the individual cows, Sapphire, Lilac, Dream Hips, Dippy and Awkward Cow.

'I'll never make no milkmaid,' he grumbled as he came across carrying the pail of milk. 'Howdy,' he greeted Zacchaeus. 'Come on in the house. I'll make some coffee, unless you'd like fresh milk instead. Lavinia!' For the first time he noticed the girl's bruised face and busted lip. 'You're hurt.'

Lavinia attempted a smile and wrote on her pad. *I tripped and fell back at the store.*

'That looks real bad. Maybe fresh milk might help instead of coffee.'

The girls followed Richard inside. Zacchaeus lingered outside. He had expected some sort of reaction when he arrived at the place that was supposed to be his home. He felt nothing as he stared around him. The homestead meant no more to him than the Circle A. Slowly he walked to the door and stepped inside.

'Richard,' Angelina said, 'this is Zacchaeus Wolfe.'

Richard had been helping Lavinia set

out the coffee mugs. He stopped what he was doing and stared at Zacchaeus. Suddenly he held out his hand.

'I heard a little about you, some good, some bad. I'm Richard Kerfoot.'

'I heard nothing but good about you, youngster. These gals have a mighty high regard for you.'

'Thank you, sir. You've had a mite of trouble I believe.'

'Hear tell you had a mite of trouble yourself. Got made homeless.'

Richard smiled ruefully. 'Sure have. I'd like to thank you for allowing me to stay here. I'll move out today.'

Zacchaeus regarded the youngster steadily. Though the name was Kerfoot the youngster did not appear to have inherited the family's callous reputation.

'No need for that, you're welcome to stay as long as you like.'

'I kinda like it here, sir, but I feel I'm only a squatter in another man's home.'

'No matter, I got some things to tell you, Richard.'

Zacchaeus accepted a mug of coffee. Before setting out for the Wolfe homestead they had agreed that Zacchaeus would be the spokesman and tell Richard an edited version of the events of the previous night.

'Someone murdered my wife and attempted to murder me. I took a bad head injury. As a result I suffered a complete loss of memory. Not knowing who I was I took a job with Julius Stiles. Without going into too much detail, Stiles was murdered yesterday by Lazy K hands. Sheriff Harrell decided I would make a good fall guy. He slung me in jail. I broke out and unfortunately ran into your brother, Stewart, and a couple of Lazy K hands. There was a shoot-out. Stewart was badly injured. I don't know if he'll survive or not.'

Richard sat very still; his only reaction was to bite his lip. Zacchaeus sipped his coffee and waited.

'The last week or so my life has been turned upside down,' Richard said in a low voice. 'I turned a blind eye to the things that were going on around me. Samuel Launder has been coming over to help me with this place. He has been telling me things about my family that I find hard to stomach. There were times I wanted to hit him and tell him to shut up. But in my heart I knew he was right. My own father near beat me to a pulp when I put those same views to him. He gave Stewart full rein to do what he did. Sooner or later my brother was bound to run up against someone who would stand up to him. If it weren't you it would have been someone else.'

'Mr Wolfe, I can't say it sits easy with me that you hurt my brother. I'll gather my things together and leave this place though it grieves me to do so.' Richard stood up and moved to the door. 'Matter of fact, I ain't got much to pack anyway. I can leave straightaway.'

It was too much for Angelina. She jumped to her feet.

'Shall I tell you why Zacchaeus

tangled with your brother?'

Lavinia grabbed at Angelina, shaking her head violently, but the girl was not to be silenced.

'Lavinia didn't fall. She got those injuries when your precious brother attacked her. And while he was trying to rape her, his two friends were attacking me. Only Zacchaeus came along when he did we might not have survived the attack.'

'It's not true?' Richard's face had gone pale as he spoke.

'They followed us home last night after we had been out here,' Angelina bore on relentlessly. 'When Zacchaeus intervened, your big brave Stewart cowered behind Lavinia and shoved a gun on her. He threatened to shoot her if Zacchaeus didn't back off. Zacchaeus took a chance and shot Stewart anyway. Stewart's buddies then tried to gun down Zacchaeus. Those cowards are rotting in hell now!'

28

Slowly the youngster came back and slumped in a chair. No one spoke for a long moment.

'Stewart was a bit wild but he wouldn't attack no females,' Richard ventured eventually.

'What about the day he held us up on the trail?' Angelina answered. 'He was trying to drag Lavinia out of the buggy when she pulled a gun on him. I reckon he was biding his time to get his revenge for being humiliated by her. He has a reputation for violence.'

Richard was staring down at his hands. 'I . . . I remember something,' he said slowly. 'What day was your aunt killed?'

'It was a few days afore the funeral, Tuesday as far as I remember. It was the Lazy K cowboys who found her. They rode into town and waited for the sheriff and his posse so as they could inform him about the killing. Sheriff Harrell sent word to us the undertaker was on his way to collect the body. He knew Lavinia was related.'

'Tuesday my brother came home alone. He was covered in blood. We thought he had been injured but he said it was chicken blood. One of the fellas played a prank and splashed him with the blood. He changed out of that outfit and told one of the hands to burn the clothes. He rode back into town.' Slowly Richard raised his head and stared round him.

'Damn me!' Zacchaeus could not help himself. 'You think Stewart had something to do with my wife's death?'

'I don't know. I'm only telling you what happened.'

'Lavinia and I did wonder why Barrett Kerfoot put up the reward to catch Zacchaeus, alive or dead.' Angelina said. 'Sheriff Harrell seemed awful keen to pin the crime on him.'

'So the sheriff knew all along about

Stewart's involvement in the murder,' Zacchaeus mused. 'That's why they were so keen to finish me off and go to the bother of hiding my body in the hills. So long as folk thought I was on the run after murdering my wife it would deflect the blame from Stewart Kerfoot. The only trouble is no one will ever believe that version of things. If only I could remember what happened to me.'

Lavinia scribbled in her notepad. *Why don't you have a look around the house? Maybe something will spark off.*

Zacchaeus nodded. Wearily he rose from his chair. He felt stiff and sore, the wound in his side was painful.

'I found a holster and pistol in a chest.' Richard seemed to have recovered from his upset at hearing about the true nature of his brother. 'There were some other things in there.' Richard led the way into a bedroom. 'I been sleeping in here.'

He opened a large tin chest and extracted a holster and a gun. He offered them up. Zacchaeus took them and belted the gun in place. Richard seemed to notice the missing hand for the first time.

'Damn me, that's what that was for.'

He rummaged some more and held out a heavy metal object with leather straps dangling. The thing looked like a cannon shell. Zacchaeus stared with some fascination at the artefact. Slowly he reached out and took the object. For a long moment he stared at it. Then he shrugged out of his jacket. With quick practised movements he attached the metal to his wrist. The mitt fitted snugly. He pressed a small stud in the side. There was a loud click and a slim lethal blade snapped into view.

'Whew,' Richard exclaimed. 'That looks dangerous.'

He looked up into the older man's face. Zacchaeus was not seeing him. His eyes were glazed over. Flashes of memory were streaking like meteorites across the darkness of his mind. He saw a man holding out the metal paw and instructing him in its use. A woman was looking seriously at him. She was very beautiful with large luminous dark eyes.

Go hunting in the hills. I don't want you here when they come looking for you.

'No . . . no . . . no . . . ' Zacchaeus moaned aloud. 'Not Gabrielle!' He sank to his knees his head bowed. 'Gabrielle . . . ' he whispered. 'I should have been here when they came. Oh, Gabrielle . . . '

To Richard's consternation Zacchaeus keeled over and lay on the floor, holding his head in his hands and moaning softy.

'Zacchaeus, Zacchaeus.'

Someone was calling him. He looked up and saw her looking down on him.

'Gabrielle,' he said, 'I'm back . . . '

'Zacchaeus, it's Angelina, Angelina and Lavinia. You must have fainted.'

Slowly the mists cleared. He stared up at the concerned faces hovering above him.

'I remember . . . I remember, but I

wish I did not. Tell me how she died.'

'All we know she was beaten to death,' Angelina said. 'She was brought to town in a closed coffin. They advised us not to view the body.'

Someone had lifted him on the bed. He pulled himself upright, winced as the pain in his wound caught him. He felt light-headed and sounds echoed in his ears. He swung his legs on to the floor. Angelina was on one side of him and Lavinia on the other, supporting him. They escorted him into the main room of the cabin. Richard was standing by the window looking miserable. He eased on to a chair. Lavinia kept her arm around him. He patted her hand.

'I'll be all right now. Let me sit awhile.'

Her pad was on the table. *Do you want to be alone?*

'Stay where you are. I just need a moment to recover. When I strapped on the mitt everything came flooding back.'

He noticed the blade was still exposed. There was a medallion on his gunbelt. He used it to depress the blade. He took hold of his niece's hand.

'Lavinia, I believe I must be cursed. The people I love are being plucked from me one by one. You and Angelina are all that are left. Even the man I went to work for was gunned down. No one is safe around me. I am a portent of death. There is a verse in the Bible that describes me for what I am. *For his house inclineth unto death and his paths unto the dead.*'

29

'I want the man who did this.'

Barrett Kerfoot was standing looking down at his son. Martha Kerfoot was sitting by the bedside sobbing quietly. Stewart's head was heavily bandaged. Only his nose and eyes were visible. The small area of skin exposed was marble white like that of a corpse.

In the corridor outside his two sons were waiting. Ethan was sharp-featured with the tan of an outdoorsman. He sported a black bushy moustache and range clothes. He ran the ranch for his dad, looking after the livestock and keeping the Lazy K cowboys employed.

Daniel was there too. Studying to be a lawyer, he had been hastily summoned from his studies. He was a tall rakish young man with carefully groomed hair. The suit he wore was of good quality though it was dusty from his travels.

Once he had learned of the crisis in the family he had taken the overnight stage to Consul.

'Go in and take a good look at your brother. Doc says until he wakes up he don't know how much damage has been done. One thing's for sure he'll never fork a horse again, or a woman for that matter. That's what some sonovabitch did to him. Keep that in mind when we catch up with him.' Barrett Kerfoot rubbed a large hand across his face before continuing. 'I need to talk to Sheriff Harrell. Doc's sedated him so he'll be out for a while. He's promised to call me when he's awake. The only ones left of Stewart's buddies are Joe McDonald and George Rankin. Damn me, this is some mess. Sheriff Harrell laid low with a spike in his eye, four of my ranch hands dead and Stewart lying in there as might be dead.' He stared hard at his two sons. 'We're gonna get whoever done this. I'll have him horsewhipped till there's no flesh left on his bones afore I hang the sonovabitch.'

'Don't worry, Pa. We'll catch up with him. He can't hide from us.'

'Humph!' Barrett Kerfoot stomped down the hallway. 'You'll find me over at the jail.'

Joe McDonald and George Rankin were huddled together talking when the boss of the Lazy K walked in. They looked nervous and worried.

'How's Stewart, Mr Kerfoot?'

'Not good,' Kerfoot answered. 'Doc don't know if he'll survive or not.' He slumped heavily into the chair at the desk. 'What the hell's this?' A ruined leather glove stuffed to make it appear solid lay on the desk.

'We found it back there under the bunk, boss.'

'What does it mean?'

'That sodbuster as Stewart had the fight with had one hand missing. When Sheriff Harrell put the handcuffs on that new man as was working for the Circle A he musta been wearing this

240

damned thing. That's how come he slipped the cuffs.'

'What are you trying to tell me?'

The two men glanced uneasily at each other, each hoping the other would speak first.

'Damn you, spit it out!'

They told him then, their own version of events. Barrett Kerfoot was no fool. He had not built up a cattle empire without having a certain amount of native shrewdness. In the middle of the narrative Ethan and Daniel came in. Their pa motioned them to silence. The two men stepped to the rear of the room and listened.

'There's something don't add up, here. Who really killed that homesteader woman?'

The men he was interrogating looked nervous. They shuffled their feet and looked at anything but at the fierce man behind the desk.

'Tell me!' As he spoke the rancher slammed his hand on the desktop. The sound was like a small explosion in the silence of the room. McDonald and Rankin jumped.

'It was an accident. The woman attacked Stewart with a hoe. Stewart was only defending himself.'

For long moments Barrett Kerfoot stared at the two frightened men. 'Tell me everything and I want the truth this time.'

So they told him about the clash with Zacchaeus Wolfe in town. How Stewart had instructed the sheriff to go after the sodbuster and arrest him. About finding the sodbuster on the trail and the fight with him. How the sheriff had organized the disposal of the injured man out in the hills. And how Stewart had gone to the sodbuster's house on the pretence of searching for him.

'Julius Stiles took on a new helper. Stewart found him out mending fences. He busted Stewart's head with the hammer and shot up the two men with him. He came in the Elephant for a drink. Stewart sent for Sheriff

Harrell to arrest him. The fella jumped the sheriff and tried to escape. Steve Hewitt and Jacob Birch were waiting outside. When all the shooting was over Hewitt, Birch and Stiles were all dead. Sheriff Harrell got the drop on Stiles's new helper. He put the cuffs on and took him down the jail.'

'You reckon this fella as Stiles had working for him is this sodbuster, Wolfe, come back from the dead?'

'It's the only explanation, boss. We didn't recognize him at first 'cause of the beard he'd growed.'

'Maybe you're right. Two men with a grudge against the Lazy K with only one hand is too much of a coincidence. It makes sense for him to work for Stiles. He knows Stewart will come after him for working for Stiles. So he bides his time and then takes his revenge. Who else knows about Stewart killing this Wolfe woman?'

'No one, boss. Stewart swore us all to secrecy. It's only Stewart and us as knows the truth. Everyone else believes the sodbuster killed his wife and then went on the run.'

'Good, keep it that way. You breathe a word of this to anyone and I'll gut-shoot you myself. Wait outside. I want a word with my boys.'

When the door closed behind the two subdued cowboys Barrett beckoned his sons over.

'Listen carefully,' he said in a low tone. 'You heard what those two rannies said. When all this is over I want them dead. They're the only witnesses as can tie Stewart in with the killing of that homestead woman. I havta find out if Sheriff Harrell is in on it too. I want no one left alive who can point the finger at your brother.'

The two Kerfoot boys nodded agreement. Almost as a reflex action they both pushed their hands down and rested them on the butts of the guns nestling on their hips.

'Your brother Paul has compassion-ate leave from the army. He should arrive sometime this morning. As soon as everything's in place we ride out to the Wolfe place. That seems as good a place as any to start our search for this troublemaker.'

30

'One thing I havta do is ride over to the Circle A and face Anna Stiles. I doubt if anyone bothered to go out there to tell her what happened to her husband.'

Zacchaeus got painfully to his feet. The soreness in his wound pulled raggedly at him, making him wince.

'You're in no fit state to ride anywhere.' Angelina objected.

'I gotta go. I owe the woman that much. Richard, will you give me directions.'

'Why don't I drive you over in the buggy?' Richard suggested. 'That's gotta be less onerous than forking a horse, and less chance of you getting lost.'

While Richard harnessed up the buggy the girls hugged Zacchaeus.

'You take care now.'

'The womenfolk seem a mite fond of

you,' Richard observed as the buggy rattled along the uneven trail.

'No more than I am of them. Family is important. You miss your family?'

'Yeah, I suppose I do. My ma most of all; my brothers too. I know we all suspect Stewart of killing your wife but he was always OK with me. Maybe it was some sorta accident.'

'Maybe. Last night when he was attacking Lavinia it were no accident. He had half her dress tore afore I came on the scene.'

Richard was quiet for a long time after this. It was Zacchaeus who broke the silence.

'Lavinia tell you how come she lost her voice?'

'No. I never did get round to asking.'

'Well then, I ain't gonna tell you neither except it were a similar sorta thing as Stewart was doing. The men as attacked her slashed her throat so bad the vocal cords were severed. They left her for dead. It's a miracle she survived.'

'Dear God, that's terrible! Why didn't she tell me?'

'You figger it out.'

There was another long silence before Richard spoke again. 'The men as did that to Lavinia, were they ever caught?'

'Yeah, they were.'

'I'm glad. Did they hang?'

'No, they didn't hang.'

'They in prison, then?'

'Boot Hill. Someone slashed their throats.'

Richard looked sideways at his companion. Zacchaeus sat staring stonily ahead. The youngster did not ask any more questions. He began to speculate what breed of man was uncle to the young woman he was so much in love with.

Anna Stiles was waiting outside the house when the buggy drew up. Zacchaeus had a dull feeling in his guts when saw her.

'Ray, what is it? Has something happened to Julius?'

'Mrs Stiles, this is the worst kind of news I could bring. Julius was shot yesterday.'

Her face was pale as she stared at him. 'Is he . . . was he badly hurt . . . ?'

Zacchaeus nodded gravely. 'There's no way I can make this any easier. I'm afraid Julius was shot dead.'

'Oh no! Not my Julius.' Her face crumpled and the tears flowed.

Zacchaeus took her arm and guided her inside. Richard tied up the team and followed them. Anna Stiles was sitting in a rocker, sobbing. When Richard entered she looked up at him, dabbed at her eyes and struggled to her feet.

'Where are my manners? I have visitors and I never even offered you a drink.'

The coffee was simmering and she busied herself for a few moments, pouring, asking if Richard wanted honey or molasses in his coffee.

'Mrs Stiles, this is Richard Kerfoot.'

She looked up at the name but

smiled a greeting through her tears. By the time she had served up the drinks she was more composed.

'How did it happen, Ray?'

'Afore I tell you that, ma'am, let me tell you something about myself. I ain't Ray Daniels. I was wounded in the head and lost my memory.' Zacchaeus pulled aside the hair that had grown over his wound. 'Today I found out who I truly was. My name is Zacchaeus Wolfe. I own a small homestead not far from here. Richard here has been minding it for me while I was away.'

'Wolfe? Wasn't there a Wolfe who murdered his wife? Julius told me about it. There was a reward out for him.'

'Yes, ma'am, that was me. I was framed. Someone else murdered my wife.' He glanced at Richard but did not elaborate. 'Them fellas I had the run-in out on the boundary fence the other day decided to ambush me. Julius was caught in the crossfire. Even though there were plenty of witnesses Sheriff Harrell decided to frame me for the killing. Thanks to your efforts at making me a false hand I managed to bust outa jail.'

'Thanks to me ... ? I don't understand.'

Zacchaeus held up the steel mitt now on the end of his wrist. A leather cover disguised the real nature of the material. 'When Sheriff Harrell put the handcuffs on me it never occurred to him that one hand was detachable. Mind you, I had one helluva job to rip the thing off. Your durable sewing almost defeated me.'

She managed a faint smile through her tears. 'But the sheriff will be after you. Have you come here to hide out?'

Zacchaeus shook his head. 'No, ma'am. My sole purpose in coming here was to bring you the bad news and see if there was anyway I could help. You can't stay out here on your own. Is there anyone you could go to?'

'No, Ray ... sorry, Zacchaeus. There's no one, only my family back East.' her voice faltered and she almost broke down again. 'What am I going to do?'

'My niece, Lavinia and her friend Angelina are back at my place. Why don't you return with us? They'll help you out. It'll give you time to grieve and decide what you want to do.'

'Oh Julius, why did this have to happen to you?' Anna Stiles was whispering as if she were actually asking her dead husband why he had gone and got himself killed. She looked up at the two men. 'What about the ranch? I just can't abandon that.'

'Don't you worry about that for now, Mrs Stiles,' Richard said. 'We'll get some help. In spite of all that's happened there are good people around here.'

While Anna Stiles gathered together a few belongings for the journey Zacchaeus collected his saddle along with his rifle. He had left it at the Circle A when he went into Consul on that fateful trip with Julius.

So much had happened and so many

were dead. The traumatic pain of his memory recovery was still acute. He wondered whether it would have been better not to remember, but rather to stay in blithe ignorance of the things he had lost.

31

Paul Kerfoot stepped down from the coach and spotted his brothers waiting for him. They greeted each other with quick, hard handshakes.

'Where's Pa?'

'He's down at the sheriff's office.'

As they walked Paul was brought up to date. 'We gotta keep Joe McDonald and George Rankin under wraps. They know things we don't wanna get out. I'll let Pa explain. We're waiting for Sheriff Harrell to wake from the sleepers Doc gave him. Pa wants to know if Harrell can tell us about all that's happened.'

'Stewart?'

'It's bad, Paul. He ain't ever gonna be right again. Sonabitch shot half his face away. It woulda have been kinder to put a bullet in his brain as leave him like that.'

'Ma?'

'Broken-hearted. You know Stewart was her favourite.'

Colonel Paul Kerfoot was a big man, even taller than his brothers. He had taken on the coarse looks of his father. He was lean and fit from his years in the army. There was another year of his service to go. He had not told his father but he was tempted to sign on for another term. Army life suited his stern nature.

Killing came natural to him. The army gave him scope for that. The Indian wars were at their height. Killing Injuns was a sport, not a chore. He would sort out this little bother thing for his pa and then go back to killing Injuns.

The greeting for his father was the same as for his brothers; a brief handshake, then down to business. George Rankin and Joe McDonald looked on. They had heard tales of the soldier son but never met him before today.

'Where's Ma?'

'She's with Stewart. You wanna go see him?'

Paul Kerfoot nodded. He was wearing civilian clothes, not wanting to draw attention to his soldierly status. In his woollen pants and cotton shirt with buckskin jacket, he looked big and imposing.

'I'll take you. I'm waiting for news about Sheriff Harrell. Sonabitch stuck a spike in his eye. Doc had to put him to sleep while he took it out. Should be awake by now. You boys stay here.'

Barrett Kerfoot nodded meaningfully to his sons. They would stay at the jail and keep watch on the only two witnesses to Gabrielle Wolfe's murder. Barrett Kerfoot did not want anything to happen to the men till he was ready to deal with them himself.

As father and son walked Barrett told Paul what was happening.

'Why ain't you going after this Wolfe fella, Pa?'

'Son, there's things must be cared for

first. Your brother Stewart went and killed that sodbuster's wife. The only witnesses are under our protection till this thing is resolved. I worry that Sheriff Harrell knows about Stewart's involvement in the killing. Before we go anywhere I gotta know and if necessary silence the sheriff. The sodbuster will keep. He might run but we'll track him down.'

'Let me take care of it, Pa. You wait on Harrell and I'll take Ethan and Daniel. Rankin and McDonald can tag along. When we taken care of the sodbuster we'll do the same with those cowboys. We can always claim they were killed in the fight with the sodbuster.'

'No! I want that sonovabitch for myself. I'm glad you're here, Paul. Of all my sons you're the one with the guts. I can't wait for you to come home from the army and take over the ranch. I guess I'm getting old. When I was younger this mess would never have happened. If you'd been here you'd have sorted it out before it got this far.

That sodbuster would be dead and buried and my son wouldn't be lying on his deathbed.'

By now they had reached the doctor's house.

'Pa, don't worry. I'll take care of everything. Stewart will be avenged.'

'Go in and see your brother. I can't bear to look at my boy lying there like a corpse. I'll wait in the hall for you. When you're done we'll go and see the sheriff together.'

When Paul Kerfoot saw his mother she was sitting in the chair with her arms and shoulders resting on the bed alongside her son. She was fast asleep. The flesh of her face sagged as she slept. Paul did not disturb her. He was shocked by how much she had aged.

When he looked at his brother a great rage swelled in him. He had seen many injured men and dead men too. Many of them he had slain himself.

He had killed Indian braves, he had killed their womenfolk, he had killed their children. He had plucked papooses from their mothers and dashed their brains out. But to see his own brother lying near death's door broke something inside him. The anger welled.

'I will get him, Stewart. He will suffer more than he could ever believe. I have learned a lot from the Indian. There are ways to do a man to death that takes a long time, a long time of suffering and agony. You will be avenged, Stewart Kerfoot. This I swear.'

He tiptoed from the room leaving the pair undisturbed. The next visit was less harrowing. Sheriff Saul Harrell, though a lawman, was really just an employee of his father's. Harrell was sitting up in bed, the top of his head swathed in bandages. Only one eye was left exposed.

'Howdy, Mr Kerfoot. Doc says I may loose my eye but hey, I got one good one.' The smile was too cheerful. 'That's funny, I can see two of you, Mr Kerfoot.'

'No, Sheriff, this is my son Paul. I ain't two.'

'Yeah, two! How come you never told me there were two of you?' Sheriff Harrell began to giggle. 'You can't fool me, Kerfoot.'

'Sheriff,' Barrett began carefully, 'we come to ask you what happened the other night when you were injured. Who did that to you; I mean damage your eye?'

'Stewart did it.'

'Stewart! You sure about that?'

Sheriff Harrell raised his finger and pointed to his good eye. There was a smirk on his face.

'Your Stewart is a good man.' Suddenly Harrell took on a worried look. 'Stewart never came to see me. I thought he might have been in to visit.'

'Sheriff, did Stewart ever kill anyone?'

'Yeah, he sure did.'

'Who did he kill?'

'He killed that sonovabitch sod-buster.'

'Did he ever kill a woman?'

'Naw, Stewart never killed no woman.' A sly look came into the sheriff's one exposed eye. 'There was one female he was dead keen on, that dressmaker female. He was allus going on about her. Mrs Kerfoot shopped there and Stewart allus went along. He reckoned that dummy woman was mad keen on him. Said he was biding his time to get to know her.'

Barrett Kerfoot was frowning. 'The dressmaker! Martha said she was a dummy. What the hell did Stewart see in her?'

'She's a looker all right. I guess Stewart just wanted a bit of fun with her. You know young'uns, they like to play around.'

Paul Kerfoot was plucking at his father's sleeve. 'The man's a fool. That spike musta gone in his brain and did some damage in there. We needn't worry about him no way.'

'Damn that sodbuster! Damn him to hell and back! He has a lot to answer for!'

They gathered their horses and rode out of Consul on the vengeance trail. In the lead was the head of the family,

Barrett Kerfoot. His three sons rode with him, Paul the soldier, Daniel the lawyer, and Ethan the straw boss of the Lazy K. With them rode Joe McDonald and George Rankin. The two cowboys unaware they were under sentence of death for having witnessed the murder of the sodbuster woman at the hands of Stewart Kerfoot.

The man they were seeking was also under sentence of death. He had shot down four of the Lazy K riders and disabled a crooked lawman. These crimes paled into insignificance when set against the wounding of Stewart Kerfoot. For that crime alone Zacchaeus Wolfe must die — the slower and more painfully the better.

32

Samuel Launder pulled up at the Wolfe homestead. Angelina came out and when she saw the visitor her face lit up.

'Samuel, how good to see you.'

Samuel's broad smile showed his own pleasure at seeing Angelina. 'Howdy, Miss Angelina,' he said in his shy slow way. 'Sure good to see you.'

Lavinia came out on the porch to stand beside Angelina.

'We're waiting for Richard to come back. I thought that was him.'

'I saw a bunch of riders a while back. Too far away to see right who they were.'

'It wouldn't be Richard. He was driving the buckboard. We've good news, Samuel. Zacchaeus Wolfe has come back.'

'That is real good news, indeed.' Samuel climbed down from the cart.

For a moment he stood, looking down at his feet and not knowing where to put his hands. 'I brung you something, Miss Angelina.'

'Oh Samuel, you are so kind. What is it?'

The homesteader turned, reached into the cart and produced a leather belt. It was adorned with silver studs and glittered in the sunlight as he held it out to her. Angelina's eyes were shining as she took the gift.

'Oh, Samuel it's beautiful. I'll try it on now.'

Quickly the girl buckled the belt in place. Slowly she pirouetted.

'What do you think, Lavinia? Isn't it beautiful?'

Lavinia clapped her hands in appreciation. Angelina stopped whirling and taking Samuel by surprise flung her arms around the youth and hugged him tightly. Samuel flushed bright red. He blinked in surprise and pleasure. His big hands hung by his sides. He did not know what to do in the face of this unexpected gesture. Angelina laughed delightedly and spun away from him.

'Come in the house, Samuel.'

As she turned to the cabin she observed Lavinia peering at something in the distance. Lavinia was using her hand to shade her eyes. Angelina and Samuel both turned to look. At the same time the sound of hoof beats reached them. They watched with some concern as the riders pulled up outside the cabin.

'That's Barrett Kerfoot, Richard's father, and his brothers. What do they want here?'

The riders edged their mounts closer into the yard, completely surrounding the people standing there. Every rider had a pistol in his hand. It was a frightening and menacing display. The three youngsters drew closer together. Without preamble Barrett Kerfoot spoke.

'We're looking for Zacchaeus Wolfe.'

It was Angelina who answered. 'There's no one of that name here.'

'Where is he?'

'What do you want him for?' Angelina was trying to overcome her apprehension. It was a daunting sight for the youngsters to be confronted by six armed hostile men.

'I'll ask the questions. But if you must know he's a fugitive from justice. We're here to take him in.'

'There's no one here. We haven't seen Mr Wolfe for weeks.'

Barrett turned his head. 'Search the place.'

The Kerfoot boys climbed down to do his bidding. The three youngsters in the yard drew closer together.

'You're wasting your time,' Angelina said though there was a tremor in her voice as she spoke.

Barrett ignored her. He pointed at Samuel with his pistol. 'Who're you?'

'I'm a neighbour, just drove over to see if these ladies needed any help.'

The men were spilling from the cabin. 'Nothing.'

'When's he due back?'

'When's who due back?' Angelina was stalling for time hoping the men would get fed up and ride away again.

Barrett climbed down from his mount and issued a stream of orders.

'Get them in the cabin. Ethan, you get the horses out of sight. Take them over that mound and make sure you tie them secure. I don't want to go chasing after horses if we have to take off sharp. Stay up there and keep a look out. You see anyone coming you holler.'

'What are you doing?' Angelina blustered. 'This is private property!'

'Get her inside. Tie them up if you have to.'

'No!' Samuel planted his big frame in front of Barrett. The youngster was the same height as the rancher but much more muscular and solid.

Paul Kerfoot was near the two men, having just come from searching the cabin. His arm rose and fell. There was a solid clunk as his gun connected with the homesteader's head. Samuel grunted and went down.

'Samuel!' Angelina screamed as she rushed forward.

Paul Kerfoot grabbed Angelina, twisted her about and gave her a vicious shove towards the cabin. Angelina stumbled and went down on her knees. Lavinia was instantly by her side helping her upright.

'If you don't get in that cabin now so help me I'll shoot that thick-headed sodbuster,' Paul snarled.

The girls were too frightened not to obey. All thoughts of defying these brutal men were quashed by the sudden violence.

'Lug that piece of shit out of sight.'

Joe McDonald and George Rankin dragged the unconscious youth around the corner of the building.

'Everyone inside. When that sonovabitch arrives back here I don't want him to see anything amiss. We'll take him completely by surprise. Ethan will give us plenty of warning.'

The two frightened women were herded inside. Paul Kerfoot came behind, taking great pleasure in mercilessly pushing them forward. They stumbled inside, feeling the cruel jabs of his heavy-handed herding. In a short time the yard of the little homestead lay deserted except for Samuel's cart with the pony standing patiently in the harness.

'Get making some coffee,' Paul Kerfoot ordered the women. He seemed to enjoy frightening them. 'Any trouble from you and you'll be lying outside with your heads staved alongside your hard-headed sodbuster friend.'

Seeing nothing to be gained from not complying Angelina and Lavinia did as they were told. As she worked Lavinia felt the weight of the pocket gun she always carried. It was a pathetic defence against the might of the six brutal men who had so suddenly taken over the peaceful homestead.

Angelina fretted about Samuel. The youngster had tried to stand up for her and Lavinia. Now he lay outside with a busted skull. Angelina ached to go to him and minister to him. She knew such a request would bring a brutal refusal. The kettle had not quite boiled when there came a shrill whistle from outside.

'Get them females on the floor. A peep outta them and you got my permission to bash their heads in.'

The order was swiftly and brutally carried out. Angelina and Lavinia were pushed roughly to the floor. Paul Kerfoot hunkered beside them. He held his pistol in his hand.

'Please call out,' he begged them. 'I'm just aching to find out if female heads is as soft as I believe.'

Colonel Paul Kerfoot knew quite well that female skulls crushed just as easily as male ones. At the end of a raid on a camp his sabre would be red with the gore of both females and males. Slashing down on the unprotected head of a running quarry was great sport. It gave a superior feeling of power to kill from the top of a galloping horse.

Seeing these females lying before him created a killing urge he was finding hard to contain. He reached out and stroked Lavinia's dark tresses. The girl shuddered beneath his touch.

33

Richard was driving the buggy. Beside him sat Anna Stiles. She had packed a carpetbag, now stored in the back along with Zacchaeus and his saddle. The newly widowed woman was sitting slumped in her seat beside Richard. The youngster's desultory attempts at conversation eventually trailed off. They travelled the journey mostly in silence.

Zacchaeus lay in the rear wedged between the saddle and the well-stuffed carpetbag. He was extremely uncomfortable. His wound burned. The binding his niece had wound around his chest to keep the cotton dressing in place seemed to constrict his breathing. He felt hot and uncomfortable and not inclined to talk.

In some ways he felt responsible for the death of Julius Stiles. If the Lazy K cowboys had not been gunning for him

Julius would have in all probability not have been caught in the crossfire.

Sunk in his dire thoughts, Zacchaeus was not taking much notice of where they were. It came as a surprise when Richard spoke to Anna Stiles.

'Almost there, ma'am. You'll like Lavinia and Angelina.'

'I'm sure I will, Richard. I been thinking, it seems strange for a Kerfoot to be helping someone like me. After all the Lazy K has been causing trouble for a long time.'

'Mrs Stiles, I don't like some of the things my family was up to. When I confronted my father about it he threw me off the Lazy K. Zacchaeus has kindly let me stay at his place for now. I was minding it while he went missing. Now it looks as if I gotta look for another position.'

There was silence as Anna Stiles thought about this.

'I don't suppose you would think of running a small ranch name of Circle A?'

Richard shot a startled look at the woman beside him. 'Mrs Stiles, I figured you would be selling up after what has happened. Ain't you afraid to stay out there now?'

'Julius brought me out here because he thought it would improve my health. In spite of all the trouble he had with the Lazy K we were happy. I feel I would be letting Julius down if I were to sell up and go back home to my folks. Julius will be buried here and here I'll stay to be near him.'

'Ma'am, I'd be right honoured to take on the job. It's one thing I know about, is ranching.'

'I . . . there's not much money. Julius was always figuring ways to balance the books. I don't right know how I'll be able to pay you.'

'Ma'am, don't worry about that. Right now I have nothing. A roof over my head, a job and good supper at the end of a hard day's work is all the reward I need.'

Anna Stiles could not help it. At the

end of this speech she burst into sobs. Richard looked nonplussed.

'Ma'am, I sure am sorry if what I said offended you. I don't mean I'm a charity case, or that you are, for that matter. I just meant the arrangement would more 'n likely suit us both.'

She put her hand out and squeezed his arm, but was too full of emotion to say anything. Richard didn't know how to respond. They drove on in silence.

'Looks like Samuel is visiting,' he observed as he caught sight of the cart in front of the building. 'You'll like Samuel, ma'am. He's a good honest soul.'

Zacchaeus was silent during this exchange. He was thinking the arrangement just brokered between Richard and Anna Stiles might work out well for both of them. Anne had recovered well from the shock of her husband's death. So much so that she was making plans to carry on in the face of the tragedy. Such is the resilience of the human spirit.

He was congratulating himself on the decision to drive across to the Circle A. The couple in the front seat were resolving their problems without any help from him. He tried to ease his cramped position. Agony stabbed through him. He decided to stay where he was till they pulled up at the cabin. It would be an embarrassment to ask for help but he would if needs be.

The approach to his home brought back the acute pain of the loss of his wife. Compared to mental pain of this tragedy the physical discomfort from his stiffening wound was but a pinprick. He closed his eyes as the ache of the bereavement welled inside him.

'I should have been here,' he whispered, so low it was not heard above the rattle of the buggy.

And then the buggy stopped.

'Here we are,' Richard told Anne. 'I don't know where everyone is. But they won't have gone far.'

He jumped down to help the woman from the buggy. Zacchaeus climbed painfully down to join them, his wound stiff and unyielding. Then Zacchaeus noticed the open window and the barrel of a gun poking part way through. A man stepped outside and stood on the porch, a revolver held in his hand. He was a big man wearing a buckskin jacket.

'Mister, there's a half a dozen guns aimed at you. Move a muscle and we'll be scraping the remains off the side of that buggy.'

Zacchaeus stayed where he was. Richard whirled round to confront the speaker.

'Paul, what in tarnation you doing here?'

'Hello, little brother, I hear you gone native.'

As the brothers greeted each other Daniel Kerfoot emerged from the doorway, also with a drawn gun. Next came Barrett Kerfoot.

'We got your women inside with one of my men holding a gun on them. You give us any trouble they have orders to shoot them.' The rancher turned and called into the cabin. 'Joe, go round the back and call Ethan down. We got the wolf in the trap.'

Joe McDonald came out and, looking scared, scuttled round the back. They could hear him calling to Ethan.

'Pa, what the hell's going on?'

'Stay where you are, traitor! I told you before you ain't no son of mine.'

'Well, I sure wouldn't want to be part of a family who makes war on women. Let those females go. They ain't part of this.'

While he was speaking Richard ignored the guns pointed in his direction and moved towards the cabin. Barrett Kerfoot's gun came up to cover his son. Paul Kerfoot was nearer. He swung his pistol against the youngster's head. With a sudden cry Richard stumbled to his knees. That was when Zacchaeus moved.

When Paul shifted position to bludgeon his brother he came between his father's drawn gun and Zacchaeus.

Daniel was to one side. Zacchaeus guessed Paul was the most dangerous of the Kerfoot family. If he put him down he might stand a chance of saving the remaining members of his family.

Zacchaeus launched himself at Paul. The big soldier was slightly off balance as he struck his young brother. Zacchaeus hit him with his shoulder and Paul Kerfoot stumbled sideways. His feet became entangled with Richard and he tripped, going down with his attacker on top.

Zacchaeus gritted his teeth as his wound felt as though it had split open again. In spite of the pain he might have managed to disable Paul Kerfoot and taken on the rest of the family had not Ethan Kerfoot at that moment come round the corner of the cabin. He moved swiftly and rammed his revolver against the neck of the man on top of his brother.

'Ease off, or you're dead, sodbuster!'

34

Zacchaeus went very still. Paul Kerfoot stared up at the man who had put him down. His face was twisted up in anger.

'You heard my brother, sodbuster! Very carefully move off me. Ethan, put a hole in him if he moves any faster than a tortoise.'

There was nothing Zacchaeus could do. Carefully he stood up. Paul Kerfoot came up with him. With sudden viciousness he drove his fist into Zacchaeus. Zacchaeus gasped, doubled over and staggered back. He crashed against the buggy.

'Pa, Ethan, keep him covered. Daniel, you and McDonald take an arm apiece and hold him up. I guess its time to soften up this hardcase.'

They spread-eagled Zacchaeus against the side of the buggy, the lawyer on one side and the hired hand on the other, Paul holstered his pistol and stepped up to face him.

'You caused us so much grief, sodbuster. Gunned down Lazy K men. Put our sheriff out of action. Shot my brother, Stewart. That was a bad mistake, mister. But your worst mistake was coming back here. When you killed your wife you should have kept on going.'

His fist shot out, taking Zacchaeus in the midriff. Zacchaeus grunted and sagged against the men holding him. He was trying to draw in his breath when the fist hit him again.

'Stop it, damn you! He didn't kill his wife. It was Stewart as killed her.'

Richard was on his feet swaying unsteadily. Blood was leaking down the side of his face. For a moment there was stillness in that yard. The Kerfoot family were shocked into silence by Richard's outburst. Everyone's attention was on the youth. Paul was momentarily distracted from the punishment of the troublemaker by his brother's revelation of the thing the family wanted kept under wraps.

The big soldier was standing in a boxer's stance his legs wide apart to give him a solid base for punching. It was a mistake to take his eye off the target. Zacchaeus let the men on each side take his weight. His foot lashed out. The kick went deep, crushing soft tissue. The stricken man went down, his gasp of agony audible in the empty silence of the yard. Colonel Paul Kerfoot curled in the dirt almost unable to breathe as the white-hot hot pain lanced through his groin.

'Damn you!'

Daniel Kerfoot let go of his captive's arm and clawed for his holstered pistol. Joe McDonald, on the other side, was not so ready to act. He was immobile with shock as he stared at Paul Kerfoot writhing in agony on the ground.

Zacchaeus punched Joe McDonald in the side of the head with his metal fist. Joe lost all interest in Paul. He slid down the side of the buggy and lay half underneath.

Daniel had his pistol out. A bullet from Barrett Kerfoot splintered the buggy beside Zacchaeus. He reached out and pulled the lawyer close, at the same time grabbing for the lawyer's pistol. More shots rang out and Daniel stiffened against Zacchaeus as the bullets hammered into his back.

'Damn . . . ' was all the lawyer managed as he relinquished his grip on the pistol.

With the pistol in one hand Zacchaeus held on to the dying man in a desperate embrace. Barrett Kerfoot, realizing what he had done, had stopped firing at Zacchaeus. Using the dying lawyer as a shield Zacchaeus fired two shots towards the rancher with Daniel's gun. One hit him in the chest and one hammered into his guts. Barrett slammed back against the wall of the cabin. With a surprised look on his face he slid down to sit on the porch his back against the wall.

The only Kerfoot remaining immediately in the fight was Ethan. With a quickness that stunned everyone he made a grab at Mrs Stiles who, during all this, had been crouching in terrified paralysis by the front wheel of the buggy.

'Drop the gun, sodbuster, or I blow her head off.'

Daniel Kerfoot had stopped breathing. Zacchaeus relaxed his hold and the dead lawyer slid from his grasp. The gun was still in his hand as Ethan shouted again.

'Drop it, I said!'

Zacchaeus stared into Anna Stiles's face and saw the terror there. *I already as good as killed her husband*, he thought, *I can't allow her to die also*.

'OK.'

He let the gun fall. The gun had belonged to Daniel Kerfoot. It dropped back into his lap. Still holding Anna Stiles as a shield, Ethan took a quick look across at Barrett Kerfoot.

'Pa, you hit? How bad is it?'

'I'm hurt bad, son. The sonovabitch got me in the guts. It sure hurts like hell. Kill the sonovabitch.'

'Damn you!'

Ethan Kerfoot was almost weeping as he swore at Zacchaeus. He pushed Anne away and lined up to shoot. At that moment Paul recovered enough to start getting to his feet. Zacchaeus flung himself at the big soldier. Ethan fired. Something smashed Zacchaeus on the shoulder and he grunted with the sudden shock.

The two men landed in the dirt with Zacchaeus partly shielded by the bigger man. With a quick motion he activated the hidden blade in his metal mitt. Grabbing Paul by the chin he whipped the man's head round. At the same time jammed the blade against the soldier's neck with sufficient force to drive it in just a fraction.

'Don't move or you're a dead man,' he hissed.

Paul Kerfoot went very still as the steel punctured his skin. Dark blood leaked down on his shirt collar.

'Let's call it quits, Kerfoot,' Zacchaeus called. 'You got one of your family dead and your pa wounded. I can add your brother's name to the roll-call if you want to play it that way.'

It was stalemate. Paul Kerfoot would die if his brother played it wrong. The big soldier could feel the rigid hold the man had on his head. The keen blade was held steady, almost an inch deep in his neck.

'Do as he says, Ethan. Pa's bad hurt. We got to get help.'

He did not mention his own fear. Killing defenceless savages was one thing; being on the end of a vengeful sodbuster's blade was another matter all together.

Ethan hesitated. He desperately wanted to kill the sodbuster who had wreaked such havoc on his family. He glanced from Paul to his father, uncertain. Then George Rankin came to his aid.

'Hold it. I got these females here.'

First Lavinia then Angelina were pushed outside. George Rankin stepped up behind them. He had a pistol in his hands.

'I'll shoot them if I havta.'

35

Ethan Kerfoot stared with sudden triumph at Zacchaeus holding his brother in that deadly grip.

'Rankin, I'm counting to five. If the sodbuster don't give up Paul unharmed, shoot the black girl first. In fact shoot them both anyway.'

'Stop it, Ethan!' Richard called out, his voice hoarse with despair. 'Finish this now. Do as Zacchaeus says and walk away.'

'One . . . ' Ethan began his count, ignoring his brother's plea. 'Two . . . Make your choice, sodbuster, two dead females or a quick bullet in the head from me. Three . . . '

'You're all cowards!' yelled Richard. 'My big tough family hiding behind female skirts when doing their fighting.'

'Shut your mouth, Richard. I'll shoot you as soon as these sodbusters. You made your choice. You're one of them now. Pa was right. You ain't no Kerfoot.'

'I'm glad. I'd be ashamed to be part of such a cowardly family.'

'Four.'

The bellow of rage and the sudden pounding of feet on the veranda startled everyone. Samuel Launder hurtled along at the speed of a maddened steer towards George Rankin. The cowboy hardly had time to turn to see what was coming when Samuel cannoned into him.

Ethan, startled though he was by the sudden attack, kept his nerve. He snapped off a shot at the enraged youngster, but Rankin had gone down under the fierce attack and the fighters were so entangled Ethan could not get a clear shot.

Zacchaeus did the only thing he could do. He plunged the length of sharp blade on the end of his artificial hand into Paul Kerfoot's neck. The soldier shuddered as the knife went in, slicing his jugular. Blood spouted out from his throat in a rapid jet. Paul was gagging and coughing with wide-open eyes, staring in terror at his brother, Ethan.

As the soldier's lifeblood spouted on to the dirt Zacchaeus rolled towards Daniel Kerfoot. The lawyer's gun was still lying in the dead man's lap. Desperately fighting against the agony of his wounds Zacchaeus clawed for the weapon.

The flurry of movement brought Ethan's attention back from the fight on the porch. It was only then he saw what had happened to Paul. The sight of the geyser of blood spurting into the dirt of the yard from his brother's ruined throat momentarily stunned him.

'Paul!' he screamed.

Ethan's hesitation was enough to gain Zacchaeus precious seconds. He had the gun in his hand and was lining up before Ethan turned his attention towards him. Zacchaeus fired from where he lay in the dirt. Ethan was hit in the chest. He staggered back but kept hold of his pistol. Zacchaeus fired a second time. Ethan was hit again. He shuddered but managed to return a shot. Then Zacchaeus fired a third shot and Ethan went over backwards. He hit the dirt. His legs twitched momentarily, then were still.

Zacchaeus was struggling to get to his feet. The bullet in his shoulder grated on the bone. He groaned in agony but forced himself to keep moving. The fight between Samuel and George Rankin was still in progress. He had to rescue the youngster from Rankin.

The cowboy's gun went off as he tried to bring it round to bear on his attacker. Samuel was punching Rankin and at the same time trying to force the gun away. Suddenly Lavinia took a hand.

She delved into her skirt pocket and came up with the pocket gun. It was two steps to the struggling men. Her hand rose once, then again as she smashed the butt on Rankin's head. The cowboy grunted and suddenly ceased fighting. His eyes glazed over. Lavinia was ruthless. She struck again and the cowboy collapsed on the boards of the porch.

A terrible silence descended on the small yard. Zacchaeus struggled to his feet. He looked around at the devastation wrought in the yard that once he called home.

Ethan Kerfoot lay spread-eagled on his back with his Colt still clutched in his hand, his chest a bloody ruin. His brothers Paul and Daniel were curled up in postures of death. Against the cabin rested the bloated form of Barrett Kerfoot, blood pooling on the boards of the porch as he slowly bled to death.

A groan from behind Zacchaeus drew his attention to the man he had clubbed. Joe McDonald was slowly recovering. Zacchaeus quickly disarmed the cowboy. He could not repress a grunt of pain as the wound in his shoulder joined the one in his ribs in sending agony through his battered body.

Richard Kerfoot was gazing dazedly round him at his slaughtered family. Slowly the realization of what had occurred sunk in. With a sudden gasp he bent over and vomited into the dirt of the yard.

Zacchaeus walked forward. Samuel stood upright breathing heavily.

'Thank you, Miss Lavinia . . .' he got no further. Angelina flung her arms around him.

'My hero, you saved us all.'

'Angelina, I did nothing much,' stuttered Samuel, 'I think Zacchaeus did it all.'

Still holding the pistol he had taken from Joe McDonald, Zacchaeus walked slowly towards the cabin.

'Thank God you're all safe. I would never have forgiven myself if anything had happened to you. It was a mistake to leave you on your own.'

Lavinia came down and wrapped her arms around him. He looked over her shoulder at Angelina. She was standing with her arm around Samuel in a very possessive manner. The youngster looked dazed but happy. There were footsteps behind him. Zacchaeus whirled round, the gun in his hand coming up instinctively. He relaxed as he saw it was Richard Kerfoot. The youngster's distraught gaze was directed at Lavinia.

'Can you ever forgive me, Lavinia? It was my family. I take full responsibility.'

Lavinia's eyes were pools of compassion as she looked at Richard. She held out her hands. The youngster stumbled forward and took her hands in his. Then they were in each other's arms.

Zacchaeus tossed the gun into the dirt. Once more he gazed around at the bodies in his yard. Then his eyes lit on Anna Stiles. She was by the buggy with a terrified look on her face. Slowly he crossed the yard to her.

'Come in to the house, Mrs Stiles. These are the men as were responsible for the murder of your husband and my wife. In some rough way justice has been done.'

She came with him, clutching at his arm. As they mounted the step to the cabin he tried to shield her from the blood-soaked body of Barrett Kerfoot slumped on the porch.

'*For his house inclineth unto death and his paths unto the dead,*' he muttered as he ushered the woman inside his home.

THE END

THE GUN HAND

Robert Anderson

Johnny Royal had lived on his wits and his gun after leaving home following a foolish argument. Returning home, however, he finds the neighbourhood is threatened by rustlers and outlaws. He meets a local rancher, the beautiful Sarah, whose uncle's past criminal deeds have returned to haunt them. Now, Johnny, Sarah and the ranch foreman must blaze a path of destruction against the forces searching for her uncle's ill-gotten gains, in the teeth of the outlaw's meanest gunslingers.

TOO MANY SUNDOWNS

Jake Douglas

Chance Benbow thought he had found the place — and the woman — which would bring him peace and quiet and a future. But then it all blew up in his face. When he recovered from the bullet wounds, he saw his future clearly, albeit clouded by gunsmoke. He would stride through it with a gun in each hand — and if hell waited on the other side, then he would meet it head-on, taking a lot of dead men with him.